OLIVER TWIST

Charles Dickens

CONTENTS

Oliver Twist

I

BIRTH AND EARLY CHILDHOOD OF OLIVER TWIST

IN A certain town, which for many reasons it will be prudent to refrain from mentioning by name, there is a workhouse; and in this workhouse was born the item of mortality whose name is prefixed to the head of this chapter. There was nobody by but a pauper old woman who was rendered rather misty by an unwonted allowance of beer, and a parish surgeon.

As Oliver gave his first cry, the patchwork coverlet which was carelessly flung over the iron bedstead, rustled; the pale face of a young woman was raised feebly from the pillow, and a faint voice imperfectly articulated the words, 'Let me see the child, and die.'

The surgeon rose, and advancing to the bed's head, said with more kindness than might have been expected of him: 'Oh, you must not talk about dying yet.'

'Lor bless her dear heart, no!' interposed the nurse, hastily depositing in her pocket a green glass bottle, the contents of which she had been tasting in a corner with evident satisfaction. 'Lor bless her dear heart, when she has lived as long as I have, sir, and had thirteen children of her own, and all on 'em dead except two, and them in the wurkus with me, she'll know better than to take on in that way, bless her dear heart! Think what it is to be a mother, there's a dear lamb, do.'

Apparently this consolatory perspective of a mother's prospects failed in producing its due effect. The patient shook her head, and stretched out her hand towards the child.

The surgeon deposited it in her arms. She imprinted her cold white lips passionately on its forehead, passed her hands over her face, gazed wildly round, shuddered, fell back—and died. They chafed her breast, hands and temples; but the blood had stopped for ever.

'It's all over, Mrs. Thingummy!' said the surgeon at last. 'She was a good-looking girl, too. Where did she come from?'

'She was brought here last night,' replied the old woman, 'by the overseer's order. She was found lying in the street. She had walked some distance, for her shoes were worn to pieces; but where she came from, or where she was going to, nobody knows.'

The surgeon leaned over the body, and raised the left hand.

'The old story,' he said, shaking his head: 'no wedding-ring, I see. Ah! Good night!'

Oliver cried lustily. If he could have known that he was an orphan, left to the tender mercies of churchwardens and overseers, perhaps he would have cried the louder.

The parish authorities magnanimously and humanely resolved that the child should be 'farmed', or, in other words, that he should be despatched to a branch workhouse some three miles off, where twenty or thirty other juvenile offenders against the poor-laws rolled about the floor all day, without the inconvenience of too much food or too much clothing, under the parental superintendence of an elderly female, who received the culprits at, and for the consideration of seven-pence halfpenny per small head per week.

It cannot be expected that this system of farming would produce any very extraordinary or luxuriant crop. Oliver Twist's ninth birthday found him a pale, thin child, somewhat diminutive in stature and decidedly small in circumference. He was keeping this day of celebration in the coal-cellar with a select party of two other young gentlemen, who, after participating with him in a sound thrashing, had been locked up for atrociously presuming to be hungry, when Mrs. Mann, the good lady of the house, was unexpectedly startled by the apparition of fat Mr. Bumble, the beadle, striving to undo the wicket of the garden gate.

'Goodness gracious! Is that you, Mr. Bumble, sir?' said Mrs. Mann, thrusting her head out of the window in well-affected ecstasies of joy.

'Mrs. Mann, I come on business, and have something to say.'

Mrs. Mann ushered the beadle into a small parlour with a brick floor, placed a chair for him, and officiously deposited his cocked hat and cane on the table before him. Mr. Bumble wiped from his forehead the perspiration which his walk had engendered, glanced complacently at the cocked hat, and smiled.

'Now, don't you be offended at what I'm a-going to say,' observed Mrs. Mann, with captivating sweetness. 'You've had a long walk, you know, or I wouldn't mention it. Now, will you take a little drop of somethink, Mr. Bumble?'

'What is it?' inquired the beadle.

'It's gin. I'll not deceive you, Mr. B. It's gin.'

Mr. Bumble swallowed half the glass.

'And now about business,' said the beadle, taking out a leathern pocket-book. 'The child that was half-baptized Oliver Twist is nine year old today.'

'Bless him!' interposed Mrs. Mann, inflaming her left eye with the corner of her apron.

'And notwithstanding a offered reward of ten pound, which was afterwards increased to twenty pound,' said Bumble, 'we have never been able to discover who is his father, or what was his mother's settlement, name, or condition.'

Mrs. Mann raised her hands in astonishment, but added after a moment's reflection, 'How comes he to have any name at all, then?'

The beadle drew himself up with pride, and said:

'I inwented it.'

'You, Mr. Bumble!'

'I, Mrs. Mann. We name our foundlings in alphabetical order. The last was a S—Swubble, I named him. This was a T—Twist, I named *him*. The next one as comes will be Unwin, and the next Vilkins. I have got names ready made to the end of the alphabet, and all the way through it again when we come to Z.'

'Why, you're quite a literary character, sir!' said Mrs. Mann.

The beadle, evidently gratified with the compliment, finished the gin-and-water, and added,

'Oliver being now too old to remain here, the board have determined to have him back into the house. I have come out myself to take him there. So let me see him at once.'

Oliver was led into the room by his benevolent protectress.

'Will you go along with me, Oliver?' said Mr. Bumble.

Oliver was about to say that he would go along with anybody with great readiness but, catching sight of Mrs. Mann's furious countenance, he had sense enough to make a feint of feeling great regret at going away. Then, with a slice of bread in his hand, and the little brown-cloth parish cap on his head, Oliver was led away by Mr. Bumble from the wretched home where one kind word or look had never lighted the gloom of his infant years. And yet he burst into an agony of childish grief as the cottage gate closed after him. Wretched as were the little companions in misery he was leaving behind, they were the only friends he had ever known; and a sense of his loneliness in the great wide world sank into the child's heart for the first time.

Oliver had not been within the walls of the workhouse a quarter of an hour when Mr. Bumble informed him that the board had said he was to appear before it forthwith.

Not having a very clearly defined notion of what a live board was, Oliver was rather astounded by this intelligence. He had no time to think about the matter, however; for Mr. Bumble conducted him into a large whitewashed room, where eight or ten fat gentlemen were sitting round a table. At the top of the table, seated in an arm-chair rather higher than the rest, was a particularly fat gentleman with a very round, red face.

'Bow to the board,' said Bumble. Oliver, seeing no board but the table, fortunately bowed to that.

'What's your name, boy?' said the gentleman in the high chair.

Oliver was frightened at the sight of so many gentlemen, and the beadle gave him another tap behind, which made him cry. These two causes made him answer in a very low and hesitating voice, whereupon a gentleman in a white waistcoat said he was a fool. Which was a capital way of raising his spirits and putting him quite at his ease.

'Boy,' said the gentleman in the high chair, 'listen to me. You know you've got no father or mother, and that you were brought up by the parish, don't you?'

'Yes, sir,' replied Oliver, weeping bitterly.

'Well! You have come here to be educated and taught a useful trade,' said the red-faced gentleman in the high chair.

'So you'll begin to pick oakum tomorrow morning at six o'clock,' added the surly one in the white waistcoat.

Oliver bowed low by the direction of the beadle, and was then hurried away to a large ward, where, on a rough, hard bed, he sobbed himself to sleep. What a noble illustration of the tender laws of England! They let the paupers go to sleep!

Poor Oliver! He little thought, as he lay asleep in happy unconsciousness of all around him, that the board had that very day arrived at a decision which would exercise the most material influence over all his future fortunes. But they had. And this was it:

They contracted with the waterworks to lay on an unlimited supply of water, and with a corn-factor to supply periodically small quantities of oatmeal, and issued three meals a day of this thin gruel, with an onion twice a week and half a roll on Sundays.

The room in which the boys were fed was a large stone hall, with a copper at one end, out of which the master, dressed in an apron for the purpose, and assisted by one or two women, ladled the gruel at mealtimes. Of this festive composition each boy had one porringer, and no more— except on occasions of great public rejoicing, when he had two ounces and a quarter of bread besides. The bowls never wanted washing. The boys polished them with their spoons until they shone again; and then they would sit staring at the copper with such eager eyes as if they could have devoured the very bricks of which it was composed. Boys have generally excellent appetites. Oliver Twist and his companions suffered the tortures of slow starvation for three months; at last they got so voracious and wild with hunger that a council was held; lots were cast who should walk up to the master after supper that evening and ask for more; and it fell to Oliver Twist.

The evening arrived; the boys took their places. The master in his cook's uniform, stationed himself at the copper; his pauper assistants ranged themselves behind him; the gruel was served out, and a long grace was said over the short commons. The gruel disappeared; the boys whispered to each other and winked at Oliver, while his next neighbours nudged him. Child as he was, he was desperate with hunger, and reckless with misery. He rose from the table, and advancing to the master, basin and spoon in hand, said, somewhat alarmed at his own temerity:

'Please, sir, I want some more.'

The master was a fat, healthy man, but he turned very pale, and clung for support to the copper. The assistants were paralysed with wonder, the boys with fear.

'What!' said the master at length, in a faint voice.

'Please, sir,' replied Oliver, 'I want some more.'

The master aimed a blow at Oliver's head with a ladle, pinioned him in his arms, and shrieked aloud for the beadle.

The board were sitting in solemn conclave when Mr. Bumble rushed into the room in great excitement, and addressing the gentleman in the high chair said:

'Mr. Limbkins, I beg your pardon, sir! Oliver Twist has asked for more!'

There was a general start. Horror was depicted on every countenance.

'For *more*!' said Mr. Limbkins. 'Compose yourself, Bumble, and answer me distinctly. Do I understand that he asked for more after he had eaten the supper allotted by the dietary?'

'He did, sir,' replied Bumble.

'That boy will be hung,' said the gentleman in the white waistcoat. 'I know that boy will be hung.'

An animated discussion took place. Oliver was ordered into instant confinement; and a bill was next morning pasted on the outside of the gate, offering a reward of five pounds to anyone who would take Oliver Twist off the hands of the parish. In other words five pounds and Oliver Twist were offered to any man or woman who wanted an apprentice to any trade, business, or calling.

For a week after the impious and profane offence of asking for more, Oliver remained a close prisoner in the dark and solitary room to which he had been consigned by the wisdom and mercy of the board.

It chanced one morning, while Oliver's affairs were in this auspicious and comfortable state, that Mr. Gamfield, chimney-sweep, went his way down the High Street, deeply cogitating in his mind his ways and means of paying certain arrears of rent for which his landlord had become rather pressing. Passing the workhouse, his eyes encountered the bill on the gate.

'Wo-o!' said Mr. Gamfield to the donkey.

He walked up to the gate to read the bill.

The gentleman with the white waistcoat was standing at the gate with his hands behind him, after having delivered himself of some profound sentiments in the board-room. He saw at once that Mr. Gamfield was exactly the sort of master Oliver Twist wanted. Mr. Gamfield smiled too, as he perused the document; for five pounds was just the sum he'd been wishing for. So, touching his fur cap in token of humility, he accosted the gentleman in the white waistcoat.

'This here boy, sir, wot the parish wants to 'prentice,' said Mr. Gamfield.

'Ay, my man,' said the gentleman in the white waistcoat, with a condescending smile. 'What of him?'

'If the parish vould like him to learn a light, pleasant trade, in a good 'spectable chimbley-sweepin' bisness,' said Mr. Gamfield, 'I wants a 'prentice, and I am ready to take him.'

'Walk in,' said the gentleman in the white waistcoat.

Mr. Gamfield followed the gentleman in the white waistcoat into the room where Oliver had first seen him.

'It's a nasty trade,' said Mr. Limbkins, when Gamfield had again stated his wish.

'Young boys have been smothered in chimneys before now,' said another gentleman.

'That's acause they damped the straw afore they lit it in the chimbley to make 'em come down again,' said Gamfield. 'Boys is wery obstinit, and wery lazy, gen'lmen, and there's nothink like a good hot blaze to make 'em come down with a run.'

The board then proceeded to converse among themselves for a few minutes, but in so low a tone, that the words 'saving of expenditure,' 'looked well in the accounts,' 'have a printed report published,' were alone audible. These only chanced to be heard indeed, on account of their being very frequently repeated with great emphasis.

At length the whispering ceased; and the members of the board having resumed their seats and their solemnity, Mr. Limbkins said:

'We have considered your proposition and we don't approve of it.'

As Mr. Gamfield did happen to labour under the slight imputation of having bruised three or four boys to death already, it occurred to him that the board had, perhaps, in some unaccountable freak, taken it into their heads that this extraneous circumstance ought to influence their proceedings. It was very unlike their general mode of doing business, if they had.

'So you won't let me have him, gen'lmen?' said Mr. Gamfield pausing near the door.

'No,' replied Mr. Limbkins; 'at least, as it's a nasty business, we think you ought to take something less than the premium you offered.'

Mr. Gamfield's countenance brightened.

'What'll you give, Gen'lmen? Come! Don't be too hard on a poor man. What'll you give?'

'I should say, three pound ten was plenty,' said Mr. Limbkins.

The bargain was made. Mr. Bumble was at once instructed that Oliver Twist and his indentures were to be conveyed before the magistrate for signature and approval, that very afternoon.

In pursuance of this determination, little Oliver, to his excessive astonishment, was released from bondage and ordered to put himself into a clean shirt. He had hardly achieved this very unusual gymnastic performance, when Mr. Bumble brought him, with his own hands, a basin of gruel and the holiday allowance of two ounces and a quarter of bread. At this tremendous sight Oliver began to cry very piteously.

'Don't make your eyes red, Oliver, but eat your food and be thankful,' said Mr. Bumble, in a tone of impressive pomposity. 'You're going to made a 'prentice of, Oliver.'

'A 'prentice, sir!' said the child, trembling. The tears rolled down his face, and he sobbed bitterly.

On their way to the magistrate, Mr. Bumble instructed Oliver that all he would have to do would be to look very happy, and say, when the gentleman asked him if he wanted to be apprenticed, that he would like it very much indeed. When they arrived at the office he was shut up in a little room by himself, and admonished by Mr. Bumble to stay there until he came back to fetch him.

There the boy remained, with a palpitating heart, for half an hour. At the expiration of which time Mr. Bumble led him into an adjoining room, the door of which was open. It was a large room, with a great window. Behind a desk, sat two old gentlemen with powdered heads, one of whom was reading the newspaper while the other was perusing, with the aid of a pair of tortoise-shell spectacles, a small piece of parchment which lay before him. Mr. Limbkins was standing in front of the desk on one side, and Mr. Gamfield, with a partially washed face, on the other, while two or three bluff-looking men, in top-boots, were lounging about.

'This is the boy, your worship,' said Mr. Bumble.

'Oh, is this the boy?' said the old gentleman.

'This is him, sir,' replied Mr. Bumble. 'Bow to the magistrate, my dear.'

Oliver roused himself, and made his best obeisance.

'Well,' said the old gentleman, 'I suppose he's fond of chimney-sweeping?'

'He dotes on it, your worship,' replied Bumble, giving Oliver a sly pinch to intimate that he had better not say he didn't.

'And he *will* be a sweep, will he?' inquired the old gentleman.

'If we was to bind him to any other trade tomorrow he'd run away simultaneous, your worship,' replied Bumble.

'And this man who's to be his master—you, sir—you'll treat him well and feed him and do all that sort of thing, will you?' said the old gentleman.

'When I says I will, I means I will,' replied Mr. Gamfield doggedly.

'You're a rough speaker, my friend, but you look an honest, open-hearted man,' said the old gentleman, turning his spectacles in the direction of the candidate for Oliver's premium, whose villainous countenance was a regular stamped receipt for cruelty. But the magistrate was half blind and half childish, so he couldn't reasonably be expected to discern what other people did.

'I hope I am, sir,' said Mr. Gamfield with an ugly leer.

'I have no doubt you are, my friend,' replied the old gentleman, fixing his spectacles more firmly on his nose, and looking about him for the inkstand.

It was the critical moment of Oliver's fate. If the inkstand had been where the old gentleman thought it was, he would have dipped his pen into it and signed the indentures, and Oliver would have been straightway hurried off. But, as it chanced to be immediately under his nose, it followed as a matter of course that he looked all over his desk for it without finding it; and his gaze encountered the pale and terrified face of Oliver.

'My boy!' said the old gentleman, 'you look pale and alarmed. What is the matter?'

'Stand a little away from him, Beadle,' said the other magistrate, laying aside the paper and leaning forward with an expression of interest. 'Now, boy, tell us what's the matter; don't be afraid.'

Oliver fell on his knees, and clasping his hands together, prayed that they would order him back to the dark room—that they would starve him—beat him—kill him if they pleased—rather than send him away with that dreadful man.

The old gentleman in the tortoise-shell spectacles looked at his companion; he nodded significantly.

'We refuse to sanction these indentures,' said the old gentleman, tossing aside the piece of parchment as he spoke.

'I hope,' stammered Mr. Limbkins, 'I hope the magistrates will not form the opinion that the authorities have been guilty of any improper conduct, on the unsupported testimony of a mere child.'

'The magistrates are not called upon to pronounce any

opinion on the matter,' said the second old gentleman sharply. 'Take the boy back to the workhouse and treat him kindly. He seems to want it.'

The next morning, the public were once more informed that Oliver Twist was again To Let, and that five pounds would be paid to anybody who would take possession of him.

OLIVER'S FIRST JOB

Mr. Bumble, who had been despatched by the board to make various preliminary inquiries, with the view of finding out some captain or other who wanted a cabin-boy without any friends, was returning to the workhouse when he encountered at the gate no less a person than Mr. Sowerberry, the parochial undertaker.

Mr. Sowerberry was a tall, gaunt, large-jointed man, attired in a suit of threadbare black, with darned cotton stockings of the same colour and shoes to answer. His features were not naturally intended to wear a smiling aspect, but he was in general rather given to professional jocosity. His step was elastic and his face betokened inward pleasantry, as he advanced to Mr. Bumble and shook him cordially by the hand.

'By the bye,' said Mr. Bumble, 'You don't know anybody who wants a boy, do you? A porochial 'prentis, who is at present a deadweight—a millstone, as I may say—round the porochial throat? Liberal terms, Mr. Sowerberry, liberal terms!'

'Gadso!' said the undertaker, taking Mr. Bumble by the gilt-edged lapel of his official coat; 'that's just the very thing I wanted to speak to you about. I pay a good deal towards the poor's rates.'

'Hem!' said Mr. Bumble. 'Well?'

'Well,' replied the undertaker, 'I was thinking that as I pay so much towards 'em, I've a right to get as much out of 'em as I can, Mr. Bumble; and so—and so—I think I'll take the boy myself.'

Mr. Bumble grasped the undertaker by the arm, and led him into the building. Mr. Sowerberry was closeted with the board for five minutes; and it was arranged that Oliver should go to him that evening 'upon liking'—a phrase which means, in the case of a parish apprentice, that if the master find upon a short trial that he can get enough work out of a boy without putting too much food into him, he shall have him for a term of years to do what he likes with.

When little Oliver was taken before 'the gentlemen' that evening and informed that he was to go, that night, as general house-lad to a coffin-makers, and that if he complained of his situation, or ever came back to the parish again, he would be sent to sea, there to be drowned or knocked on the head, as the case might be, he evinced so little emotion that they by common consent pronounced him a hardened young rascal, and ordered Mr. Bumble to remove him forthwith.

For some time Mr. Bumble drew Oliver along without notice or remark, but as they drew near to their destination, Mr. Bumble thought it expedient to look down and see that the boy was in good order for inspection by his new master.

'Oliver!' said Mr. Bumble.

'Yes, sir,' replied Oliver in a low, tremulous voice.

'Pull that cap off your eyes, and hold up your head, sir.'

Although Oliver did as desired he wept until the tears sprung out from between his thin and bony fingers.

'Well!' exclaimed Mr. Bumble. 'Of *all* the ungratefullest and worst-disposed boy as ever I see, Oliver, you are the——'

'No, no, sir,' sobbed Oliver, clinging to the hand which held the well-known cane. 'No, no, sir, I will be good indeed; indeed, indeed, I will, sir! I am a very little boy, sir, and it is so—so——'

'So what?' inquired Mr. Bumble in amazement.

'So lonely, sir, so very lonely!' cried the child. 'Everybody hates me. Oh, sir, don't, don't pray be cross to me!' The child beat his hand upon his heart, and looked into his companion's face with tears of real agony.

Mr. Bumble, after regarding Oliver's piteous and helpless look with some astonishment, bade him dry his eyes and be a good boy. Then once more taking his hand, he walked on with him in silence.

'Aha!' said the undertaker, when they arrived, 'that's the boy, is it?' He raised the candle above his head to get a better view of Oliver. 'Mrs. Sowerberry, will you have the goodness to come here a moment, my dear?'

Mrs. Sowerberry emerged from a little room behind the shop, and presented the form of a short, thin, squeezed-up woman, with a vixenish countenance.

'Dear me,' said the undertaker's wife, 'he's very small.' Turning to Oliver, she cried, 'Get down stairs, little bag o' bones.' With this, the undertaker's wife opened a side door and pushed Oliver down a steep flight of stairs into a stone cell, damp and dark, forming the anteroom to the coal-cellar, and denominated 'kitchen', wherein sat a slatternly girl, in shoes down at heel and blue worsted stockings very much out of repair.

'Here, Charlotte,' said Mrs. Sowerberry, who had followed Oliver down, 'give the boy some of the cold bits that were put by for Trip.'

Oliver clutched at the dainty viands that the dog had neglected, and tore the bits asunder with all the ferocity of famine.

'Well,' said the undertaker's wife, when Oliver had finished his supper, which she had regarded in silent horror and with fearful auguries of his future appetite, 'have you done?'

There being nothing eatable within his reach, Oliver replied in the affirmative.

'Then come with me,' said Mrs. Sowerberry, taking up a dim and dirty lamp, and leading the way upstairs. 'Your bed's under the counter. You don't mind sleeping among the coffins, I suppose?'

Oliver meekly followed his new mistress.

Being left to himself in the undertaker's shop, Oliver set the lamp down on a workman's bench and gazed timidly about him with a feeling of awe and dread, which many people a good deal older than he will be at no loss to understand. The shop was close and hot, the atmosphere seemed tainted with the smell of coffins. The recess beneath the counter in which his flock mattress was thrust, looked like a grave; and he wished as he crept into his narrow bed, that that were his own coffin.

Oliver was awakened in the morning by a loud kicking at the outside of the shop door.

'Open the door, will yer?' cried the voice which belonged to the legs which had kicked the door.

'I will directly, sir,' replied Oliver, undoing the chain and turning the key.

'I suppose yer the new boy, ain't yer?' said the voice through the keyhole.

'Yes, sir,' replied Oliver.

'How old are yer?' inquired the voice.

'Ten, sir,' replied Oliver.

'Then I'll whop yer when I get in,' said the voice; 'you just see if I don't, that's all, my work'us brat!' and having made this obliging promise, the voice began to whistle. Oliver drew back the bolts with a trembling hand and opened the door.

For a second or two, Oliver glanced up the street and down the street and over the way, impressed with the belief that the unknown who had addressed him through the keyhole, had walked a few paces off to warm himself; for nobody did he see but a big charity boy, sitting on a post in front of the house, eating a slice of bread and butter which he cut into wedges, the size of his mouth, with a clasp knife, and then consumed with great dexterity.

'I beg your pardon, sir,' said Oliver at length, seeing that no other visitor made his appearance; 'did you knock?'

'I kicked,' replied the charity boy.

'Did you want a coffin, sir?' inquired Oliver innocently.

At this the charity boy looked monstrous fierce; and said that Oliver would want one before long, if he cut jokes with his superiors in that way.

'Yer don't know who I am, I suppose, Work'us?' said the charity boy. 'I'm Mr. Noah Claypole, and you're under me. Take down the shutters, yer idle young ruffian!'

Oliver, having taken down the shutters, and broken a pane of glass in his efforts to stagger away beneath the weight of the first one to a small court at the side of the house in which they were kept during the day, was graciously assisted by Noah, who having consoled him with the assurance that 'he'd catch it', condescended to help him. Mr. Sowerberry came down soon after. Shortly afterwards Mrs. Sowerberry appeared. Oliver having 'caught it' in fulfilment of Noah's prediction, followed that young gentleman down the stairs to breakfast.

'Come near the fire, Noah,' said Charlotte. 'I saved a nice little bit of bacon for you from Master's breakfast. Oliver, shut that door at Mr. Noah's back, and take them bits that I've put out on the cover of the bread-pan. There's your tea; take it away to that box, and drink it there, and make haste, for they'll want you to mind the shop.'

Noah was a charity boy, but no workhouse orphan. No chance child was he, his mother being a washerwoman and his father a drunken soldier. The shop-boys in the neighbourhood had long been in the habit of branding Noah, in the public streets, with the ignominious epithets of 'leathers', 'charity' and the like; and Noah had borne them without reply. But now that fortune had cast in his way a nameless orphan at whom even the meanest could point the finger of scorn, he retorted on him with interest.

Oliver had been sojourning at the undertaker's some three weeks or a month. Mr. and Mrs. Sowerberry—the shop being shut up—were taking their supper in the little back-parlour, when Mr. Sowerberry, after several deferential glances at his wife, said:

'It's about young Twist, my dear. A very good-looking boy that, my dear.'

'He need be, for he eats enough,' observed the lady.

'There's an expression of melancholy in his face, my dear,' resumed Mr. Sowerberry, 'which is very interesting. He would make a delightful mute, my love.'

Mrs. Sowerberry looked up with an expression of considerable wonderment. It was speedily determined, therefore, that Oliver should at once be initiated into the mysteries of the trade.

The occasion was not long in coming. Half an hour after breakfast next morning, Mr. Bumble entered the shop and, supporting his cane against the counter, drew forth his large, leathern pocket-book from which he selected a small scrap of paper, which he handed over to Sowerberry.

'Aha!' said the undertaker, glancing over it with a lively countenance; 'an order for a coffin, eh?'

'For a coffin first, and a porochial funeral afterwards,'

replied Mr. Bumble, fastening the strap of the leathern pocket-book, which like himself, was very córpulent.

'Bayton,' said the undertaker looking from the scrap of paper to Mr. Bumble. 'I never heard the name before.'

'We only heard of the family night before last,' said the beadle. 'A woman who lodges in the same house made an application to the porochial committee for them to send the porochial surgeon to see a woman as was very bad. He had gone out to dinner; but his 'prentice (which is a very clever lad) sent 'em some medicine in a blacking-bottle, off-hand. But what's the consequence? Why, the husband send back word that the medicine won't suit his wife's complaint, and so she shan't take it—says she shan't take it, sir! Good, strong, wholesome medicine, as was given with great success to two Irish labourers and a coal-heaver only a week before—sent 'em for nothing, with a blackin' bottle in.'

So saying, Mr. Bumble flounced out of the shop.

'Why, he was so angry, Oliver, he forgot even to ask after you!' said Mr. Sowerberry, looking after the beadle as he strode down the street. 'Noah, look after the shop. Oliver, put on your cap and come with me.'

They walked on for some time through the most crowded and densely inhabited part of the town; and then, striking down a narrow street more dirty and miserable than any they had yet passed through, paused to look for the house which was the object of their search. It was a poky, evil-smelling hovel. The very rats, which here and there lay putrefying in its rottenness, were hideous with famine.

The undertaker mounted to the top of the first flight of stairs. Stumbling against a door on the landing, he rapped at it with his knuckles. It was opened by a young girl of thirteen or fourteen.

There was no fire in the room; but a man was crouching, mechanically, over the empty stove. An old woman, too, had drawn a low stool to the cold hearth, and was sitting beside him. There were some ragged children in another corner; and in a small recess, opposite the door, there lay upon the ground something covered with an old blanket. Oliver shuddered as he cast his eyes towards the place, and crept involuntarily closer to his master; for though it was covered up, the boy felt that it was a corpse. The undertaker, producing a tape from his pocket, knelt down for a moment by the side of the body.

The terrified children cried bitterly; but the old woman who had hitherto remained as quiet as if she had been wholly deaf to all that passed, menaced them into silence.

'She was my daughter,' said the old woman, nodding her head in the direction of the corpse and speaking with an idiotic leer, more ghastly than even the presence of death in such a place. 'Lord! Lord! Well, it is strange that I, who gave birth to her, and was a woman then, should be alive and merry now, and she lying there, so cold and stiff!'

The undertaker drew Oliver after him and hurried away.

The next day, Oliver and his master returned to the miserable abode, where Mr. Bumble had already arrived, accompanied by four men from the workhouse, who were to act as bearers. An old black cloak had been thrown over the rags of the old woman and the man; and the bare coffin, having been screwed down, was hoisted on the shoulders of the bearers and carried into the street.

When they reached the obscure corner of the churchyard in which the nettles grew, and where the parish graves were made, the clergyman had not arrived. At length, after a lapse of something more than an hour, Mr. Bumble, and Sowerberry, and the clerk were seen running towards the grave. Immediately afterwards the clergyman appeared, putting on his surplice as he came along. Mr. Bumble then thrashed a boy or two, to keep up appearances, and the reverend gentleman, having read as much of the burial service as could be compressed into four minutes, gave his surplice to the clerk and walked away again.

'Now, Bill!' said Sowerberry to the grave-digger. 'Fill up!'

'Well, Oliver,' said Sowerberry, as they walked home, 'how do you like it?'

'Pretty well, thank you, sir,' said Oliver with considerable hesitation. 'Not very much, sir.'

'Ah, you'll get used to it in time, Oliver,' said Sowerberry. 'Nothing when you *are* used to it, my boy.'

* * * *

The month's trial over, Oliver was formally apprenticed. It was a nice sickly season just at this time. In commercial phrase, coffins were looking up; and, in the course of a few weeks, Oliver acquired a great deal of experience.

He continued meekly to submit, for many months, to the domination and ill-treatment of Noah Claypole, who used him far worse than before, now that his jealousy was aroused by seeing the new boy promoted to the black stick and hatband, while he, the old one, remained stationary in muffin cap and leathers. Charlotte treated him ill because Noah did; and Mrs. Sowerberry was his decided enemy, because Mr. Sowerberry was disposed to be his friend; so between these three on one side, and a glut of funerals on the other, Oliver was not always as comfortable as the hungry pig was when he was shut up, by mistake, in the grain department of a brewery.

And now I come to a very important passage in Oliver's history. One day, Oliver and Noah had descended into the kitchen at the usual dinner hour to banquet upon a small joint of mutton, when Charlotte being called out of the way, there ensued a brief interval of time, which Noah Claypole, being hungry and vicious, considered he could not possibly devote to a worthier purpose than aggravating and tantalizing young Oliver.

'Work'us,' said Noah, 'how's yer mother?'

'She's dead,' replied Oliver. 'Don't you say anything about her to me!'

Oliver's colour rose as he said this; he breathed quickly and there was a curious working of the mouth and nostrils, which Mr. Claypole thought must be the immediate precursor of a violent fit of crying. Under this impression he returned to the charge.

'What did she die of, Work'us?' said Noah.

'Of a broken heart, some of our old nurses told me,' replied Oliver, more as if he were talking to himself, than answering Noah. Then he added sharply: 'Don't say anything more to me about her; you'd better not!'

'Better not!' exclaimed Noah. 'Well! Better not! Work'us, don't be impudent. *Your* mother too! Yer must know, Work'us, yer mother was a regular, right-down bad un.'

'What did you say?' inquired Oliver, looking up quickly.

'A regular right-down bad 'un, Work'us,' replied Noah coolly.

Crimson with fury, Oliver started up, overthrew the chair and table, seized Noah by the throat, shook him in the violence of his rage, till his teeth chattered in his head, and, collecting his whole force into one heavy blow, felled him to the ground.

A minute ago the boy had looked the quiet, mild, dejected creature that harsh treatment had made him. But his spirit was roused at last; the cruel insult to his dead mother had set his blood on fire. His whole person changed as he stood glaring over the cowardly tormentor who now lay crouching at his feet, and defied him with an energy he had never known before.

'He'll murder me!' blubbered Noah. 'Charlotte! Missus! Help! help! Oliver's gone mad! Char—lotte!'

Charlotte and Mrs. Sowerberry rushed screaming into the kitchen and set upon Oliver, while Noah rose from the ground and pommelled him behind. When they could tear and beat no longer, they dragged Oliver, struggling and shouting, but nothing daunted, into the dust-cellar and there locked him up. This being done, Mrs. Sowerberry sank into a chair and burst into tears.

'What's to be done, Charlotte?' she exclaimed. 'Your master's not at home, there's not a man in the house, and he'll kick that door down in ten minutes.' Oliver's plunges against the bit of timber in question rendered this occurrence highly probable.

'Dear, dear! I don't know, ma'am,' said Charlotte.

'Run to Mr. Bumble, Noah,' said Mrs. Sowerberry, 'and tell him to come here directly, and not to lose a minute; never mind your cap! Make haste! You can hold a knife to that black eye as you run along. It'll keep the swelling down.'

Noah stopped to make no reply, but started off at his fullest speed; and very much it astonished the people who were out walking, to see a charity boy tearing through the streets pell-mell, with no cap on his head and a clasp knife at his eye.

Noah Claypole paused not until he reached the workhouse gate.

'Why, what's the matter with the boy?' said the old pauper who opened the gate to him.

'Mr. Bumble! Mr. Bumble!' cried Noah, with well-affected dismay; and in tones so loud and agitated they not only caught the ear of Mr. Bumble himself, who happened to be hard by, but alarmed him so much that he rushed into the yard without his cocked hat.

'Oh, Mr. Bumble, sir,' said Noah: 'Oliver, sir—Oliver turned wicious. He tried to murder me, sir; and then he tried to murder Charlotte; and then missis. Oh! What a dreadful pain it is! Such agony, please, sir!' And here Noah writhed and twisted his body into an extensive variety of eel-like positions, as if suffering the acutest torture.

When he observed a gentleman in a white waistcoat crossing the yard, he was more tragic in his lamentations than ever, rightly conceiving it highly expedient to attract the notice and rouse the indignation of the gentleman aforesaid. The gentleman's notice was very soon attracted; for he had not walked three paces when he turned angrily round and inquired what that young cur was howling for.

'It's a poor boy from the free-school, sir,' replied Mr. Bumble, 'who's been nearly murdered, sir, by—young Twist. The young savage has likewise attempted to murder the female servant and his missis.'

'Please, sir,' asked Noah, 'missis wants to know whether Mr. Bumble can spare time to step up there directly, and flog him—'cause master's out.'

'Certainly, my boy, certainly,' said the gentleman in the white waistcoat, smiling benignly and patting Noah's head, which was about three inches higher than his own. 'Bumble just step up to Sowerberry's with your cane, and see what's best to be done. Don't spare him, Bumble.'

The cocked hat and cane having been adjusted to their owner's satisfaction, Mr. Bumble and Noah Claypole betook themselves with all speed, to the undertaker's shop.

Here the position of affairs had not at all improved. Sowerberry had not returned and Oliver continued to kick, with undiminished vigour at the cellar door. The accounts of his ferocity, as related by Mrs. Sowerberry and Charlotte, were of so startling a nature that Mr. Bumble judged it prudent to parley before opening the door. With this view he gave a kick at the outside, by way of prelude, then applying his mouth to the keyhole, said in a deep and impressive voice:

'Oliver!'

'Come; you let me out!' replied Oliver from the inside.

'Do you know this here voice, Oliver?' said Mr. Bumble.

'Yes,' replied Oliver.

'Ain't you afraid of it, sir? Ain't you a-trembling while I speak, sir?'

'No,' replied Oliver boldly.

'Oh, you know, Mr. Bumble, he must be mad,' said Mrs. Sowerberry. 'No boy in half his senses could venture to speak so to you.'

'It's not madness, ma'am,' replied Mr. Bumble after a few moments in deep meditation. 'It's meat.'

'What?' exclaimed Mrs. Sowerberry.

'Meat, ma'am, meat,' replied Bumble, with stern emphasis. 'You've overfed him, ma'am. You've raised a artificial soul and spirit in him, ma'am, unbecoming to a person of his condition, as the board, Mrs. Sowerberry, who are practical philosophers, will tell you. The only thing that can be done now, that I know of, is to leave him in the cellar for a day or so till he's a little starved down, and then to take him out and keep him on gruel all through his apprenticeship.'

Sowerberry returned at this juncture and unlocked the cellar door in a twinkling, and dragged his rebellious apprentice out by the collar.

Oliver's clothes had been torn in the beating he had received; his face was bruised and scratched, and his hair scattered over his forehead. The angry flush had not disappeared, however; and when he was pulled out of his prison, he scowled boldly on Noah and looked quite undismayed.

'Now, you're a nice young fellow, ain't you?' said Sowerberry, giving Oliver a shake and a box on the ear.

'He called my mother names,' replied Oliver.

'Well, and what if he did, you little ungrateful wretch?' said Mrs. Sowerberry. 'She deserved what he said, and worse.'

'She didn't,' said Oliver.

'She did,' said Mrs. Sowerberry.

'It's a lie!' said Oliver.

Mrs. Sowerberry burst into a flood of tears.

This flood of tears left Mr. Sowerberry no alternative. He at once gave the boy a drubbing which satisfied even Mrs. Sowerberry herself and rendered Mr. Bumble's subsequent application of the parochial cane rather unnecessary. For the rest of the day he was shut up in the back kitchen, in company with the pump and a slice of bread; and at night Mrs. Sowerberry ordered him upstairs to his dismal bed.

He had listened to their taunts with a look of contempt and borne the lash without a cry, but now, when there were none to see or hear him, he fell upon his knees on the floor and wept such tears as few so young ever have cause to pour out.

The candle was burning low in the socket when he rose to his feet. Having availed himself of its expiring light to tie up in a handkerchief the few articles of wearing apparel he had, he sat himself down upon a bench to wait for morning.

With the first ray of light that struggled through the crevices in the shutters, Oliver arose and unbarred the door. One timid look around—one moment's pause of hesitation— he had closed it behind him, and was in the open street.

He looked to the right and to the left, uncertain whither to fly. Following the footpath he well remembered he had trotted beside Mr. Bumble, when he first carried him to the workhouse from the farm, he walked on until he reached the house. Here he stopped and peeped into the garden. A child was weeding one of the little beds; as he stopped, he raised his pale face and disclosed the features of one of his former companions.

'Hush, Dick,' said Oliver, as the boy ran to the gate and thrust his thin arm between the rails to greet him. 'Is anyone up?'

'Nobody but me,' replied the child.

'You mustn't say you saw me, Dick,' said Oliver. 'I am running away. They beat and ill-used me, Dick; and I am going to seek my fortune some long way off. I don't know where. How pale you are!'

'I heard the doctor tell them I was dying,' replied the child with a faint smile. 'I am very glad to see you, dear, but don't stop, don't stop! Kiss me,' said the child, climbing up the low gate, and flinging his little arms round Oliver's neck. 'Good-bye, dear! God bless you!'

The blessing was from a young child's lips, but it was the first that Oliver had ever invoked upon his head; and through the struggles and sufferings and troubles and changes of his after life he never once forgot it.

A DEN OF THIEVES

OLIVER reached the stile at which the bypath terminated, and once more gained the high road. It was eight o'clock now. Though he was nearly five miles away from the town, he ran and hid behind the hedges, by turns, till noon, fearing that he might be pursued and overtaken. Then he sat down to rest by the side of the milestone and began to think, for the first time, where he had better go and try to live.

The stone by which he was seated bore, in large characters, an intimation that it was just seventy miles from that spot to London. The name awakened a new train of ideas in the boy's mind. London!—that great large place!—nobody—not even Mr. Bumble could ever find him there! He jumped upon his feet and again walked forward.

Oliver walked twenty miles that day, and all that time tasted nothing but the crust of dry bread and a few draughts of water, which he begged at the cottage doors by the road-side. When the night came he turned into a meadow and, creeping close under a hayrick, determined to lie there till morning.

He felt cold and stiff when he got up next morning, and had walked no more than twelve miles when night closed in again. His feet were sore and his legs so weak that they trembled beneath him. Another night passed in the bleak damp air, made him worse; when he set forward on his journey next morning, he could hardly crawl along.

In some villages, large painted boards were fixed up, warning all persons who begged within the district that they would be sent to jail. In fact, if it had not been for a good-hearted turnpike man and a benevolent old lady, Oliver would most assuredly have fallen dead upon the king's highway, but the old lady took pity upon the poor orphan and gave him what little she could afford.

Early on the seventh morning after he had left his native place, Oliver limped slowly into the little town of Barnet. The window shutters were closed; the street was empty; not a soul had awakened to the business of the day.

Oliver crouched, with bleeding feet and covered with dust, upon a doorstep for some time till he was roused by a boy who was surveying him most earnestly from the opposite side of the way. He was a snub-nosed, flat-browed, common-faced boy enough, and as dirty a juvenile as one would wish to see, but he had about him all the airs and manners of a man. He was short for his age, with rather bow-legs, and little, sharp, ugly eyes. His hat was stuck lightly on the top of his head. He wore a man's coat, which reached nearly to his heels. He had turned the cuffs back, half-way up his arm, to get his hands out of the sleeves.

'Hullo, my covey! What's the row?' said this strange young gentleman to Oliver.

'I am very hungry and tired,' replied Oliver, the tears standing in his eyes as he spoke. 'I have walked a long way. I have been walking these seven days.'

'Walking for sivin days!' said the young gentleman. 'Oh, I see. Beak's order, eh? A beak's a madgst'rate,' he added, noticing Oliver's look of surprise, 'and when you walk by a beak's order, it's not straight forerd, but always agoin' up, and nivir a coming down again. But come,' said the young gentleman, 'you want grub, and you shall have it.'

Assisting Oliver to rise, the young gentleman took him to an adjacent chandler's shop, where he purchased a sufficiency of ready-dressed ham and a half-quartern loaf. Taking the bread under his arm, the young gentleman turned into a small public-house, and led the way to a tap-room in the rear of the premises. Here a pot of beer was brought in, by direction of the mysterious youth, and Oliver made a long and hearty meal.

'Going to London?' said the strange boy, when Oliver had at length concluded.

'Yes.'

'Got any lodgings?'

'No.'

'Money?'

'No.'

The strange boy whistled, and put his arms into his pockets as far as the big coat sleeves would let them go.

'Do you live in London?' inquired Oliver.

'Yes, I do, when I'm at home,' replied the boy. 'I suppose you want some place to sleep in tonight, don't you?'

'I do indeed,' answered Oliver. 'I have not slept under a roof since I left the country.'

'Don't fret your eyelids on that score,' said the young gentleman. 'I've got to be in London tonight; and I know a 'spectable old genelman as lives there, wot'll give you lodgings for nothink.'

This unexpected offer of shelter was too tempting to be resisted and led to a more friendly and confidential dialogue, from which Oliver discovered that his friend's name was Jack Dawkins, and that among his intimate friends he was better known by the sobriquet of the 'Artful Dodger'.

As John Dawkins objected to their entering London before nightfall, it was nearly eleven o'clock when they reached the turnpike at Islington. They crossed from the Angel into St. John's Road, struck down the small street which terminates at Sadler's Wells Theatre, through Exmouth Street and Coppice Row, down the little court by the side of the workhouse, across the classic ground which once bore the name of Hockley-in-the-Hole, thence into Little Saffron Hill, and so into Saffron Hill the Great, along which the Dodger scudded at a rapid pace, directing Oliver to follow close at his heels.

Oliver could not help bestowing a few hasty glances on either side of the way as he passed along. A dirtier or more wretched place he had never seen. He was just considering whether he hadn't better run away, when they reached the bottom of the hill and his conductor, catching him by the arm, pushed open the door of a house near Field Lane, and drawing him into the passage closed it behind them.

'Now, then!' cried a voice from below, in reply to a whistle from the Dodger.

'Plummy and slam!' was the reply.

This seemed to be some watchword or signal that all was right, for the light of a feeble candle gleamed on the wall at the remote end of the passage, and a man's face peeped out from where a balustrade of the old kitchen staircase had been broken away.

'There's two of you,' said the man, thrusting the candle farther out, and shading his eyes with his hand. 'Who's the t'other one?'

'A new pal,' replied Jack Dawkins, pulling Oliver forward.

'Where did he come from?'

'Greenland. Is Fagin upstairs?'

'Yes, he's a-sortin' the wipes. Up with you!' The candle was drawn back and the face disappeared.

Oliver ascended with much difficulty the dark and broken stairs. His conductor threw open the door of a back room and drew Oliver in after him.

The walls and ceiling of the room were perfectly black with age and dirt. There was a deal table before the fire, upon which were a candle stuck in a ginger beer bottle, two or three pewter pots, a loaf and butter, and a plate. In a frying pan, which was on the fire, and which was secured to the mantelshelf by a string, some sausages were cooking; and standing over them with a toasting fork in his hand, was a very old shrivelled Jew, whose villainous-looking and repulsive face was obscured by a quantity of matted red hair. He was dressed in a greasy flannel gown, with his throat bare; and seemed to be dividing his attention between the frying pan and a clothes-horse, over which a great number of silk handkerchiefs were hanging. Several rough beds, made of old sacks, were huddled side by side on the floor. Seated round the table were four or five boys, none older than the Dodger, smoking long clay pipes and drinking spirits with the air of middle-aged men. These all crowded about their associate as he whispered a few words to the Jew, and then turned round and grinned at Oliver. So did the Jew, toasting fork in hand.

'This is him, Fagin,' said Jack Dawkins, 'my friend Oliver Twist.'

The Jew grinned and, making a low obeisance to Oliver, took him by the hand and hoped he should have the honour of his intimate acquaintance.

'We are very glad to see you, Oliver, very,' said the Jew.

'Dodger, take off the sausages, and draw a tub near the fire for Oliver.'

Oliver ate his share, and the Jew then mixed him a glass of hot gin-and-water, telling him he must drink it off directly because another gentleman wanted the tumbler. Oliver did as he was desired. Immediately afterwards he felt himself gently lifted onto one of the sacks, and then he sunk into a deep sleep.

It was late next morning when Oliver awoke from a sound, long sleep. There was no other person in the room but the old Jew, who was boiling some coffee in a saucepan for breakfast, whistling softly to himself as he stirred it round and round with an iron spoon.

Although Oliver had roused himself from sleep, he was not thoroughly awake. He saw the Jew with his half-closed eyes, heard his low whistling, and recognized the sound of the spoon grating against the saucepan's sides; and yet when the Jew looked at Oliver, and called him by his name, the boy did not answer, and was to all appearance asleep.

After satisfying himself upon this head, the Jew stepped gently to the door, which he fastened. He then drew forth—as it seemed to Oliver, from some trap in the floor—a small box which he placed carefully on the table. His eyes glistened as he raised the lid and looked in. Dragging an old chair to the table, he sat down and took from it a magnificent gold watch, sparkling with jewels, besides rings, brooches, bracelets, and other articles of jewellery, of such magnificent materials and costly workmanship that Oliver had no idea even of their names.

Having replaced these trinkets, the Jew took out another, so small that it lay in the palm of his hand. At length he put it down as if despairing of success, and leaned back in his chair, muttering.

His bright dark eyes fell on Oliver's face; the boy's eyes were fixed on him in mute curiosity; and although the recognition was only for an instant—for the briefest space of time than can possibly be conceived—it was enough to show the old man that he had been observed.

'Did you see any of these pretty things, my dear?' said the Jew, laying his hand upon the box after a short pause.

'Yes, sir,' replied Oliver.

'Ah!' said the Jew, turning rather pale. 'They—they're mine, Oliver; my little property. All I have to live upon in my old age. The folks call me a miser, my dear. Only a miser, that's all.'

Oliver cast a deferential look at the Jew and asked if he might get up.

'Certainly, my dear, certainly,' replied the old gentleman. 'Bring me that pitcher of water in the corner by the door and I'll give you a basin to wash in, my dear.'

Oliver got up, walked across the room, and stooped for an instant to raise the pitcher. When he turned his head, the box was gone.

He had scarcely washed himself when the Dodger returned, accompanied by a very sprightly young friend, whom Oliver had seen smoking on the previous night, and who was now formerly introduced to him as Charley Bates. The four sat down to breakfast on the coffee, and some hot rolls and ham, which the Dodger had brought home in the crown of his hat.

When the breakfast was cleared away, the merry old gentleman and the two boys played at a very curious and uncommon game, which was performed in this way: The merry old gentleman, placing a snuff-box in one pocket of his trousers, a note-case in the other, and a watch in his waistcoat pocket, with a guard-chain round his neck, and sticking a mock diamond pin in his shirt, buttoned his coat tight round him, and putting his spectacle-case and handkerchief in his pockets, trotted up and down the room with a stick, in imitation of the manner in which old gentlemen walk about the streets any hour in the day. Sometimes he stopped at the fireplace, and sometimes at the door, making believe that he was staring with all his might into shop windows. At such times he would look constantly round him, for fear of thieves, and would keep slapping all his pockets in turn, to see that he hadn't lost anything, in such a very funny and natural manner, that Oliver laughed till the tears ran down his face. All this time, the two boys followed him closely round, getting out of his sight so nimbly, every time he turned round, that it was impossible to follow their motions. At last the Dodger trod upon his toes or ran upon his boot accidentally, while Charley Bates stumbled up against him behind; and in that one moment, they took from him, with the most extraordinary rapidity, snuff-box, note-case, watch-guard, chain, shirt-pin, pocket handkerchief, even the spectacle-case. If the old gentleman felt a hand in any one of his pockets, he cried out where it was; and then the game began all over again.

When this game had been played a great many times, a couple of young ladies called to see the young gentlemen, one of whom was named Bet, and the other Nancy. They wore a good deal of hair, not very neatly turned up behind, and were rather untidy about the shoes and stockings. They were not exactly pretty.

These visitors stopped a long time. At length the Dodger and Charley and the two young ladies went away together, having been kindly furnished by the amiable old Jew with money to spend.

'There, my dear,' said Fagin. 'That's a pleasant life, isn't it? They have gone out for the day.'

'Have they done work, sir?' inquired Oliver.

'Yes,' said the Jew, 'that is, unless they should unexpectedly come across any, when they are out; and they won't neglect it if they do, my dear, depend upon it. Make 'em your models, Is my handkerchief hanging out of my pocket, my dear?' said the Jew, stopping short.

'Yes, sir,' said Oliver.

'See if you can take it out without my feeling it, as you saw them do when we were at play this morning.'

Oliver held up the bottom of the pocket with one hand, as he had seen the Dodger hold it, and drew the handkerchief lightly out of it with the other.

'Is it gone?' cried the Jew.

'Here it is, sir,' said Oliver, showing it in his hand.

'You're a clever boy, my dear,' said the playful old gentleman, patting Oliver on the head approvingly. 'I never saw a sharper lad. Here's a shilling for you. If you go on in this way, you'll be the greatest man of the time. And now come here, and I'll show you how to take the marks out of the handkerchiefs.'

Oliver was soon deeply involved in his new study.

For many days Oliver remained in the Jew's room, picking the marks out of the pocket handkerchiefs (of which a great number were brought home), and sometimes taking part in the game already described which the two boys and the Jew played regularly every morning. At length he began to languish for fresh air and entreated the old gentleman to let him go out to work with his two companions.

One morning, Oliver obtained the permission to go out he had so eagerly sought. The three boys sallied out, the Dodger with his coat sleeves tucked up, and his hat cocked as usual; Master Bates sauntering along with his hands in his pockets; and Oliver between them, wondering where they were going, and what branch of manufacture he would be instructed in first.

The pace at which they went was such a very lazy, ill-looking saunter that Oliver soon began to think that his companions were going to deceive the old gentleman by not going to work at all.

They were just emerging from a narrow court not far from the open square in Clerkenwell, which is yet called by some strange perversion of terms, 'The Green', when the Dodger made a sudden stop and, laying his finger on his lip, drew his companions back, with the greatest caution and circumspection.

'What's the matter?' demanded Oliver.

'Hush!' replied the Dodger. 'Do you see that old cove at the bookstall?'

'The old gentleman over the way?' said Oliver. 'Yes I see him.'

'He'll do,' said the Dodger.

'A prime plant,' observed Master Charley Bates.

Oliver stood looking on in silent amazement.

The old gentleman was a very respectable looking personage, with a powdered head and gold spectacles. He was dressed in a bottle-green coat with a black velvet collar, wore white trousers and carried a smart bamboo cane under his arm. He had taken up a book from the stall and there he stood, reading away, as hard as if he were in his elbow-chair in his own study.

What was Oliver's horror and alarm as he stood a few

paces off, looking on with his eyelids as wide open as they could possibly go, to see the Dodger plunge his hand into the old gentleman's pocket and draw from thence a handkerchief; to see him hand the same to Charley Bates, and finally to behold them both, running away round the corner at full speed!

In an instant the whole mystery of the handkerchief and the watches and the jewels and the Jew rushed upon the boy's mind. He stood, for a moment, and, not knowing what he did, made off as fast as he could lay his feet to the ground.

This was all done in a minute's space. In the very instant when Oliver began to run, the old gentleman, putting his hand to his pocket and missing his handkerchief, turned sharp round. Seeing the boy scudding away at such a rapid pace, he very naturally concluded him to be the depredator; and shouting 'Stop thief!' with all his might, made off after him, book in hand.

But the old gentleman was not the only person who raised the hue and cry. The Dodger and Bates merely retired into the very first doorway round the corner. They no sooner heard the cry and saw Oliver running than, guessing how the matter stood, they issued forth with great promptitude, and shouting 'Stop thief!' too, joined in the pursuit like good citizens.

The cry is taken up by a hundred voices and the crowd accumulate at every turning, all in pursuit of one wretched breathless child, panting with exhaustion. Stopped at last! A clever blow. He is down upon the pavement and the crowd eagerly gather round him.

Oliver lay, covered with mud and dust, and bleeding from the mouth, looking wildly round upon the heap of faces that surrounded him, when the old gentleman was officiously dragged and pushed into the circle by the foremost of the pursuers.

'Yes,' said the gentleman, 'I am afraid it is the boy.'

'Afraid!' murmured the crowd. 'That's a good 'un!'

'Poor fellow!' said the gentleman, 'he has hurt himself.'

A police officer (who is generally the last person to arrive in such cases) at that moment made his way through the crowd and seized Oliver by the collar.

'Come, get up,' said the man roughly.

'It wasn't me, indeed, sir. Indeed, indeed, it was two other boys,' said Oliver, clasping his hands passionately and looking round. 'They are here somewhere.'

'Oh, no, they ain't,' said the officer. He meant this to be ironical, but it was true besides; for the Dodger and Charley Bates had filed off down the first convenient court they came to. 'Come, get up!'

Oliver, who could hardly stand, made a shift to raise himself on his feet, and was at once lugged along the streets by the jacket-collar, at a rapid pace. The gentleman walked on with them by the officer's side; and as many of the crowd as could achieve the feat got a little ahead and stared back at Oliver from time to time. The boys shouted in triumph, and on they went.

4

A PLEASANT INTERLUDE

THE offence had been committed within the district, and indeed in the immediate neighbourhood of a very notorious metropolitan police office. The crown had only the satisfaction of accompanying Oliver through two or three streets and down a place called Mutton Hill, when he was led beneath a low archway and up a dirty court, into this dispensary of summary justice, by the backway. It was a small paved yard into which they turned, and here they encountered a stout man with a bunch of whiskers on his face and a bunch of keys in his hand.

'What's the matter now?' said the man carelessly.

'A young fogle-hunter,' replied the man who had Oliver in charge.

'Are you the party that's been robbed, sir?' inquired the man with the keys.

'Yes, I am,' replied the old gentleman; 'but I am not sure that this boy actually took the handkerchief. I—would rather not press the case.'

'Must go before the magistrate, now, sir,' replied the man. 'His worship will be disengaged in half a minute. Now, young gallows!'

This was an invitation for Oliver to enter through a door which he unlocked as he spoke, and which led into a stone cell. Here he was searched, and nothing being found upon him, locked up.

The old gentleman looked almost as rueful as Oliver when the key grated in the lock.

'There is something in that boy's face,' he said to himself as he walked slowly away, tapping his chin with the cover of the book in a thoughtful manner, 'something that touches and interests me. *Can* he be innocent? He looked like. . . . By the by,' exclaimed the old gentleman, halting abruptly and staring up into the sky. 'Bless my soul! Where have I seen something like that look before?'

But the old gentleman could recall no one countenance of which Oliver's features bore a trace. He was roused by a touch on the shoulder and a request by the man with the keys to follow him into the office, and was at once ushered into the imposing presence of the renowned Mr. Fang.

The office was a front parlour with a panelled wall. Mr. Fang sat behind a bar at the upper end; and on one side of the door was a sort of wooden pen in which poor little Oliver was already deposited, trembling very much at the awfulness of the scene.

Mr. Fang was a lean, long-backed, stiff-necked, middle-sized man, with no great quantity of hair, and what he had, growing on the back and sides of his head. His face was stern and much flushed.

The old gentleman bowed respectfully and, advancing to the magistrate's desk, said, suiting the action to the word, 'That is my name and address, sir.' He then withdrew a pace or two and, with another polite and gentlemanly inclination of the head, waited to be questioned.

Now it so happened that Mr. Fang was out of temper, and he looked up with an angry scowl.

'Who are you?' said Mr. Fang.

The old gentleman pointed, with some surprise, to his card.

'Officer!' said Mr. Fang, tossing the card contemptuously away with the newspaper. 'Who is this fellow?'

'My name, sir,' said the old gentleman, *speaking* like a gentleman, 'my name, sir, is Brownlow.'

'Appears against the boy, does he?' said Fang, surveying Mr. Brownlow from head to foot. 'Swear him!'

Mr. Brownlow submitted to be sworn.

'Now,' said Fang, 'what's the charge against this boy?'

'I was standing at a bookstall . . .' Mr. Brownlow began.

'Hold your tongue, sir!' said Mr. Fang. 'Policeman! Where's the policeman? Here, swear this policeman. Now, policeman, what is this?'

The policeman, with becoming humility, related how he had taken the charge, how he had searched Oliver and found nothing on his person, and how that was all he knew about it.

'Are there any witnesses?' inquired Mr. Fang.

'None, your worship,' replied the policeman.

Mr. Fang sat silent for some minutes, and then, turning round to the prosecutor, said in a towering passion,

'Do you mean to state what your complaint against this boy is, man, or do you not?'

With many interruptions and repeated insults, Mr. Brownlow contrived to state his case, observing that, in the surprise of the moment, he had run after the boy because he had seen him running away, and expressing his hope that the magistrate would deal as leniently with the boy as justice would allow. 'And I really fear he is ill,' concluded the old gentleman.

'Oh yes, I dare say,' said Mr. Fang, with a sneer. 'Come, none of your tricks here, you young vagabond; they won't do. What's your name?'

Oliver tried to reply, but his tongue failed him. He was deadly pale and the whole place seemed turning round and round. Raising his head he murmured a feeble prayer for a draught of water.

'Stuff and nonsense!' said Mr. Fang. 'Don't try to make a fool of me.'

'Take care of him, officer,' said the old gentleman, raising his hands instinctively. 'He'll fall down.'

'Let him, if he likes,' cried Fang.

Oliver availed himself of the kind permission and fell to the floor in a fainting fit.

'I knew he was shamming,' said Fang, as if this were incontestable proof of the fact: 'Let him lie there; he'll soon be tired of that. He stands committed for three months— hard labour, of course. Clear the office.'

A couple of men were preparing to carry the insensible boy to his cell when an elderly man of decent but poor appearance, clad in an old suit of black, rushed hastily into the office and advanced towards the bench.

'Stop, stop! Don't take him away! For heaven's sake stop a moment!' cried the newcomer, breathless with haste.

'What is this? Who is this?' stormed Mr. Fang. 'Turn this man out. Clear the office!'

'I *will* speak!' cried the man, 'I will not be turned out.

I saw it all, I keep the bookstall. I demand to be sworn. I will not be put down, Mr. Fang, you must hear me. You must not refuse, sir. I saw three boys, two others and the prisoner here, loitering on the opposite side of the way when this gentleman was reading. The robbery was committed by another boy, I saw it done. And I saw that this boy was perfectly amazed and stupefied by it.' Having by this time recovered a little breath, the worthy bookstall keeper proceeded to relate, in a more coherent manner, the exact circumstances of the robbery.

'Why didn't you come here before?' said Fang after a pause.

'I hadn't a soul to mind the shop,' replied the man. 'Everybody who could have helped me had joined in the pursuit.' He added that the book that Mr. Brownlow was reading had not yet been paid for.

'A nice person to prefer a charge against a poor boy!' said Fang, with a comical effort to look humane. 'I consider, sir, that you have obtained possession of that book under very suspicious and disreputable circumstances, and you may think yourself very fortunate that the owner of the property declines to prosecute. Let this be a lesson to you, my man, or the law will overtake you yet. The boy is discharged. Clear the office.'

'D——n me!' cried the old gentleman, bursting out with the rage he had kept down so long, 'd——n me! I'll——'

The indignant Mr. Brownlow was conveyed out in a perfect frenzy of rage and defiance. He reached the yard and his passion vanished in a moment. Little Oliver Twist lay on his back on the pavement with his shirt unbuttoned and his temples bathed with water, his face a deadly white and a cold tremble convulsing his whole frame.

'Poor boy, poor boy,' said Mr. Brownlow, bending over him. 'Call a coach, somebody, pray. Directly!'

A coach was obtained, and Oliver, having been carefully laid on one seat, the old gentleman got in and sat himself on the other and away they drove.

The coach rattled away, over nearly the same ground as that which Oliver had traversed when he first entered London in company with the Dodger, and, turning a different way when it reached the Angel at Islington, stopped at length before a neat house in a quiet shady street near Pentonville. Here a bed was prepared without loss of time, in which Mr. Brownlow saw his young charge carefully and comfortably deposited; and here he was tended with a kindness and solicitude that knew no bounds.

But for many days, Oliver remained insensible to the goodness of his new friends. Weak, and thin, and pallid, he awoke at last.

'What room is this? Where have I been brought to?' said Oliver. 'This is not the place I went to sleep in.'

The curtain at the bed's head was hastily drawn back, and a motherly old lady appeared.

'Hush, my dear,' said the old lady softly. 'You must be very quiet or you will be ill again, and you have been very bad—as bad as bad could be, pretty nigh. Lie down again, there's a dear!'

Oliver soon fell into a gentle doze, from which he was awakened by the light of a candle, which, being brought near the bed, showed him a gentleman with a very large and loud-ticking gold watch in his hand, who felt his pulse and said he was a great deal better.

'Just as I expected, Mrs. Bedwin,' said the doctor. 'You may give him a little tea, ma'am, and some dry toast without butter. Don't keep him too warm, ma'am, but be careful that you don't let him be too cold.'

Oliver dozed off again soon after this; when he awoke it was nearly twelve o'clock. The old lady tenderly bade him goodnight shortly afterwards, and left him in charge of a fat old woman.

It had been a bright day for hours when Oliver opened his eyes; he felt cheerful and happy. The crisis of the disease was safely past. He belonged to the world again.

In three days' time, he was able to sit in an easy chair, well propped up with pillows; and as he was still too weak to walk, Mrs. Bedwin had him carried downstairs to the little housekeeper's room which belonged to her.

'You're very, very kind to me, ma'am,' said Oliver.

'Well, never you mind that, my dear,' said the old lady. 'The doctor says Mr. Brownlow may come to see you this morning, and we must get up our best looks, because the better we look, the more he'll be pleased. Are you fond of pictures, dear?' inquired the old lady, seeing that Oliver had fixed his eyes, most intently, on a portrait which hung against the wall, just opposite his chair.

'I don't quite know, ma'am,' said Oliver, without taking his eyes from the canvas; 'I have seen so few that I hardly know. What a beautiful, mild face that lady's is! Is that a likeness, ma'am? Whose is it?'

'Why, really, my dear, I don't know,' answered the old lady in a good-humoured manner. 'It's not a likeness of anybody that you or I know, I expect. It seems to strike your fancy, dear.'

'It is so very pretty,' replied Oliver.

'Why, sure you're not afraid of it?' said the old lady, observing in great surprise, the look of awe with which the child regarded the painting.

'Oh no, no,' returned Oliver, quickly, 'but the eyes look so sorrowful; and where I sit they seem fixed upon me. It makes my heart beat,' added Oliver in a low voice, 'as if it was alive, and wanted to speak to me, but couldn't.'

'Lord save us!' said the old lady, starting, 'don't talk in that way, child. You're weak and nervous after your illness. Let me wheel your chair round to the other side, and then you won't see it. There!' said the old lady, suiting the action to the word; 'you don't see it now, at all events.'

He was given some broth and had scarcely swallowed the last spoonful when there came a soft rap at the door. 'Come in,' said the old lady, and in walked Mr. Brownlow.

'Poor boy, poor boy!' said Mr. Brownlow, clearing his throat. 'I'm rather hoarse this morning, Mrs. Bedwin. I'm afraid I've caught cold, but never mind that.' He turned to Oliver. 'How do you feel, my dear?'

'Very happy, sir,' replied Oliver, 'and very grateful indeed, sir, for your goodness to me.'

'Good boy,' said Mr. Brownlow. 'Now what are we to call you, eh?'

'My name is Oliver, sir,' replied the little invalid. 'Oliver Twist.'

'Queer name!' said the old gentleman, looking steadily at Oliver, and the old idea of the resemblance between his features and some familiar face came upon him so strongly that he could not withdraw his gaze.

'I hope you are not angry with me, sir,' said Oliver, raising his eyes beseechingly.

'No, no,' replied the old gentleman. 'Why! What's this? Bedwin, look there!'

As he spoke he pointed hastily to the picture above Oliver's head and then to the boy's face. There was its living copy. The eyes, the head, the mouth; every feature was the same. The expression was, for the instant, so precisely alike, that the minutest line seemed copied with startling accuracy.

Oliver knew not the cause of this sudden exclamation, for, not being strong enough to bear the start it gave him, he fainted away, a weakness on his part which affords the narrative an opportunity of relieving the reader from suspense in behalf of the two young pupils of the Merry Old Gentleman.

When the Dodger and his accomplished friend Master Bates had joined in the hue-and-cry which was raised at Oliver's heels, they quitted the pursuit when the general attention was fixed upon Oliver. Thereafter, making immediately for their home by the shortest possible cut through a most intricate maze of narrow streets, they slunk down their own court.

A few minutes later the noise of footsteps on the stairs roused the merry old gentleman as he sat over the fire. There was a rascally smile on his white face as he turned round, and looking sharply out from under his thick red eyebrows, bent his ear towards the door and listened.

'Why, how's this?' muttered the Jew, changing countenance, 'only two of 'em? Where's the third? They can't have got into trouble. Hark!'

The footsteps approached nearer; they reached the landing. The door was slowly opened; and the Dodger and Charley Bates entered, closing it behind them.

'Where's Oliver?' said the Jew, seizing the Dodger tightly by the collar and threatening him with horrid imprecations. 'Speak out, or I'll throttle you!'

'Why the traps have got him, and that's all about it,' said the Dodger sullenly. 'Come, let go o' me, will you?' And he swung himself, at one jerk, clean out of the big coat, which he left in the Jew's hands.

'Why, what the blazes is in the wind now?' growled a deep voice.

The man who growled out these words was a stoutly built fellow of about five and thirty, in a black velveteen coat, very soiled drab breeches, lace-up half boots, and grey cotton stockings, which enclosed a pair of legs with large swelling calves. He had a broad heavy countenance with a beard of three days' growth, and two scowling eyes, one of which displayed various particoloured symptoms of having been recently damaged by a blow.

A white shaggy dog, with his face scratched and torn in twenty different places, skulked into the room after him.

The man seated himself deliberately and addressed Fagin. 'What are you up to? Ill-treating the boys, you covetous, avaricious, in-sa-ti-a-ble ole fence. I wonder they don't murder you! *I* would if I was them. If I'd been your 'prentice I'd have done it long ago, and——'

'Hush! Hush! Mr. Sikes,' said the Jew, trembling and pointing towards the boys.

After swallowing two or three glasses of spirits, Mr. Sikes condescended to take some notice of the young gentlemen, which gracious act led to a conversation in which the cause and manner of Oliver's capture were circumstantially detailed.

'I'm afraid,' said the Jew, 'he may say something that will get us into trouble.'

'That's very likely,' returned Sikes with a malicious grin. 'If he hasn't peached and is committed, there's no fear till he comes out again, and then he must be taken care of. You must get hold of him somehow.'

The prudence of this line of action, indeed, was obvious, but unfortunately, there was one very strong objection to its being adopted. This was that the Dodger, and Charley Bates, and Fagin and Mr. William Sikes, happened, one and all, to entertain a violent and deeply rooted antipathy to going near a police office on any ground or pretext whatever. But the sudden entrance of two young ladies whom Oliver had seen on a former occasion caused the conversation to flow afresh.

'The very thing!' said the Jew. 'Bet will go, won't you, my dear?'

'Go where?' inquired the young lady.

'Only just up to the office,' said the Jew coaxingly.

The young lady expressed an emphatic and earnest desire to be 'blessed' if she would, but by dint of alternate threats, promises and bribes Nancy, the other female, was ultimately prevailed upon to undertake the commission.

Accordingly, with a clean, white apron tied over her gown, and her curl-papers tucked up under a straw bonnet—both articles being provided from the Jew's inexhaustible stock—Miss Nancy prepared to issue forth on her errand. She made the best of her way to the police office, whither, not with-standing a little natural timidity consequent upon walking through the streets alone and unprotected, she arrived in perfect safety shortly afterwards.

Entering by the back door, she tapped softly with the key at one of the cell-doors, and listened.

'Nolly, dear?' murmured Nancy in a gentle voice. 'Nolly?'

But, as neither of the criminals in the cells answered to the name of Oliver, or knew anything about him, Nancy made straight up to the bluff officer in the striped waistcoat; and with the most piteous wailings and lamentations demanded her own dear brother.

'I haven't got him, my dear,' said the old man.

'Where is he?' screamed Nancy in a distracted manner.

'Why, the gentleman's got him,' replied the officer.

'What gentleman? Oh, gracious heaven! What gentleman?' exclaimed Nancy.

In reply to this incoherent questioning, the old man informed the deeply affected sister that Oliver had been taken ill in the office, and discharged in consequence of a witness having proved the robbery to have been committed by another boy, not in custody; and that the prosecutor had carried him away, in an insensible condition, to his own residence, of and concerning which, all the informant knew was that it was somewhere in Pentonville, he having heard that word mentioned in the directions to the coachman.

Mr. Bill Sikes no sooner heard the account of the expedition delivered than he hastily called up the white dog, and, putting on his hat, expeditiously departed, without devoting any time to the formality of wishing the company good morning.

'We must know where he is, my dears; he must be found,' said the Jew, greatly excited. 'Charley, do nothing but skulk about till you bring home some news of him! Nancy, my dear, I must have him found. I trust to you, my dear—to you and the Artful for everything! Stay, stay,' added the Jew, unlocking a drawer with a shaking hand; 'there's money, my dears. I shall shut up this shop tonight. You'll know where to find me! Don't stop here a minute. Not an instant, my dears! We may stop his mouth yet.'

* * * *

Oliver soon recovering from the fainting fit into which Mr. Brownlow's abrupt exclamation had thrown him, the subject of the picture was carefully avoided both by the old gentleman and Mrs. Bedwin, in the conversation that ensued, which indeed bore no reference to Oliver's history or prospects, but was confined to such topics as might amuse without exciting him. He was still too weak to get up to breakfast; but when he came down into the housekeeper's room next day, his first act was to glance up at the wall, in the hope of again looking at the face of the beautiful lady. His expectations were disappointed, however, for the picture had been removed.

'I liked to see it,' cried Oliver. 'I quite loved it.'

'Well, well!' said the old lady good-humouredly, 'you get well as fast as ever you can, dear, and it shall be hung up again. There! I promise you that! Now let us talk about something else.'

This was all the information Oliver could obtain about the picture at that time. After tea, the old lady began to teach Oliver cribbage, which he learned very quickly, and they played with great interest and gravity, until it was time for the invalid to have some warm wine and water with a slice of dry toast, and then go cosily to bed. They were happy days, those of Oliver's recovery.

One evening, about a week after the affair of the picture,

as he was sitting talking to Mrs. Bedwin, there came a message down from Mr. Brownlow that if Oliver Twist felt pretty well, he should like to see him in his study and talk to him a little while.

Oliver tapped at the study door. On Mr. Brownlow calling to him to come in, he found himself in a little back room, quite full of books, with a window looking into some pleasant little gardens. There was a table drawn up before the window, at which Mr. Brownlow was seated reading. When he saw Oliver he pushed the book away from him and told him to come near the table and sit down.

'There are a good many books, are there not, my boy?' said Mr. Brownlow, observing the curiosity with which Oliver surveyed the shelves that reached from the floor to the ceiling.

'A great number, sir,' replied Oliver, 'I never saw so many.'

'You shall read them if you behave well,' said the old gentleman kindly. 'Now I want you to pay great attention, my boy, to what I am going to say. I shall talk to you without any reserve because I am sure you are as well able to understand me as many older persons would be.'

'Oh, don't tell me you are going to send me away, sir, pray!' exclaimed Oliver, alarmed at the serious tone of the old gentleman's commencement. 'Don't turn me out of doors to wander in the streets again. Let me stay here and be a servant. Don't send me back to the wretched place I came from. Have mercy upon a poor boy, sir!'

'My dear child,' said the old gentleman, moved by the warmth of Oliver's sudden appeal; 'you need not be afraid of my deserting you unless you give me cause. Now you say you are an orphan without a friend in the world; all the inquiries I have been able to make confirm the statement. Let me hear your story: where you come from, who brought you up, and how you got into the company in which I found you. Speak the truth, and you shall not be friendless while I live.'

Oliver was on the point of beginning to relate how he had been brought up on the farm, and carried to the workhouse by Mr. Bumble, when a peculiarly impatient little double-knock was heard at the street door, and the servant, running upstairs, announced Mr. Grimwig.

'Is he coming up?' inquired Mr. Brownlow.

'Yes, sir,' replied the servant.

'Shall I go downstairs, sir?' inquired Oliver.

'No,' replied Mr. Brownlow, 'I would rather you remained here.'

At this moment, there walked into the room, supporting himself by a thick stick, a stout old gentleman, rather lame in one leg, who was dressed in a blue coat, striped waistcoat, nankeen breeches and gaiters, and a broad-brimmed white hat, with the sides turned up with green. A very small-pleated shirt frill stuck out from his waistcoat; and a very long steel watch chain, with nothing but a key at the end, dangled loosely below it. The ends of his white neckerchief were twisted into a ball about the size of an orange; the variety of shapes into which his countenance was twisted, defy description. Holding out a small piece of orange-peel at arm's length, he exclaimed in a growling, discontented voice:

'Look here! Do you see this! Isn't it a most wonderful and extraordinary thing that I can't call at a man's house but I find a piece of this poor surgeon's-friend on the staircase. I've been lamed with orange-peel once, and I know orange-peel will be my death at last. It will, sir; orange-peel will be my death, or I'll be content to eat my own head, sir!'

This was the handsome offer with which Mr. Grimwig backed and confirmed nearly every assertion he made.

'Hullo, what's that?' he cried, looking at Oliver and retreating a pace or two.

'This is young Oliver Twist, whom we were speaking about,' said Mr. Brownlow.

Oliver bowed.

'How are you, boy?' said Mr. Grimwig.

'A great deal better, thank you, sir,' replied Oliver.

Mr. Brownlow, seeming to apprehend that his singular friend was about to say something disagreeable, asked Oliver to step downstairs and tell Mrs. Bedwin that they were ready for tea, which, as he did not half like the visitor's manner, he was very happy to do.

'He is a nice-looking boy, is he not?' inquired Mr. Brownlow.

'I don't know. I never see any difference in boys. I only know two sorts of boys. Mealy boys and beef-faced boys.'

'And which is Oliver?'

'Mealy.'

This, Mr. Brownlow, knowing his friend's peculiar ties, bore with great good humour; and as Mr. Grimwig, at tea, was graciously pleased to express his entire approval of the muffins, matters went on very smoothly and Oliver, who made one of the party, began to feel more at his ease than he had yet done in the fierce old gentleman's presence.

'And when are you going to hear a full, true and particular account of the life and adventures of Oliver Twist?' asked Grimwig of Mr. Brownlow, at the conclusion of the meal.

'Tomorrow morning,' replied Mr. Brownlow. 'I would rather he was alone with me at the time. Come up to me at ten o'clock, my dear.'

'Yes, sir,' replied Oliver.

'I'll tell you what,' whispered that gentleman to Mr. Brownlow, 'he won't come up to you tomorrow morning. I saw him hesitate. He is deceiving you, my good friend.'

'I'll swear he is not,' replied Mr. Brownlow warmly. 'I'll answer for that boy's truth with my life!'

'And I for his falsehood with my head!' rejoined Mr. Grimwig.

As fate would have it, Mrs. Bedwin chanced to bring in, at this moment, a small parcel of books, which Mr. Brownlow had that morning purchased of the identical bookstall keeper who has already figured in this history. Having laid them on the table she prepared to leave the room.

'Stop the boy, Mrs. Bedwin!' said Mr. Brownlow; 'there is something to go back.'

'He has gone, sir,' replied Mrs. Bedwin.

'Dear me, I am very sorry for that,' exclaimed Mr. Brownlow; 'I particularly wished those books to be returned tonight.'

'Send Oliver with them,' said Mr. Grimwig, with an ironical smile; 'he will be sure to deliver them safely, you know.'

Mr. Brownlow agreed, and gave Oliver some money and a message for the bookseller.

'I won't be ten minutes, sir,' said Oliver eagerly.

Having buttoned up the banknote in his jacket pocket and placed the books carefully under his arm, he made a respectful bow and left the room. Mrs. Bedwin followed him to the street door, giving him many directions about the nearest way, and the name of the bookseller, and the name of the street, all of which Oliver said he clearly understood. Having superadded many injunctions to be sure and not take cold, the old lady at length permitted him to depart.

'Bless his sweet face!' said the old lady, looking after him, 'I can't bear, somehow, to let him go out of my sight.'

At 'this moment Oliver looked gaily round and nodded before he turned the corner. The old lady smilingly returned his salutation and, closing the door, went back to her own room.

'Let me see, he'll be back in twenty minutes at the longest,' said Mr. Brownlow, pulling out his watch and placing it on the table. 'It will be dark by that time.'

'Oh! You really expect him to come back, do you?' inquired Mr. Grimwig.

'Don't you?' asked Mr. Brownlow, smiling.

'No,' he said, smiting the table with his fist, 'I do not. The boy has a new suit of clothes on his back, a set of valuable books under his arm, and a five-pound note in his pocket. He'll join his old friends and laugh at you. If ever that boy returns to this house, sir, I'll eat my head.'

With these words he drew his chair closer to the table; and there the two friends sat, in silent expectation, with the watch between them.

It grew so dark that the figures on the dial plate were scarcely discernible; but there the two old gentlemen continued to sit, in silence, with the watch between them.

5

BACK TO SQUALOR

In the obscure parlour of a low public-house in the filthiest part of Little Saffron Hill, a dark and gloomy den where a flaring gaslight burnt all day in the wintertime, and where no ray of sun ever shone in the summer, there sat Mr. William Sikes. At his feet sat a white-coated, red-eyed dog. The door opened and Fagin entered.

'Well, what have you got to say to me?' demanded Sikes of the newcomer.

'It's all passed safe through the melting-pot,' replied Fagin, 'and this is your share. Here it is, all safe!' As he spoke he drew forth an old cotton handkerchief from his breast and untying a large knot in one corner, produced a small brown paper packet. Sikes, snatching it from him, hastily opened it and proceeded to count the sovereigns it contained.

'This is all, is it?' inquired Sikes.

'All,' replied the Jew.

'Jerk the tinkler,' said Sikes.

These words, in plain English, conveyed an injunction to ring the bell. It was answered by another Jew, younger than Fagin, but nearly as vile and repulsive in appearance.

'Is anybody here, Barney?' inquired Fagin.

'Dot a shoul,' replied Barney, whose words, whether they came from the heart or not, made their way through the nose. 'Dobody but Biss Dadsy; she's bid havin' a plate of boiled beef id the bar.'

'Send her here,' said Sikes, pouring out a glass of liquor. 'Send her here.'

Barney retired and, presently returning, ushered in Nancy, who was decorated with the bonnet, apron, basket, and street-door key, complete.

'You are on the scent, are you, Nancy?' inquired Sikes, proffering the glass.

'Yes, I am, Bill,' replied the young lady, 'and tired enough of it I am, too. The brat's been ill and confined to the crib; and...'

'Ah, Nancy dear,' said Fagin, looking up and checking her with a look.

Nancy suddenly checked herself and with several gracious smiles upon Mr. Sikes, turned the conversation to other matters, declaring in about ten minutes that it was time to go. Mr. Sikes expressed his intention of accompanying her and they went away together.

Meanwhile, Oliver Twist, little dreaming that he was within so very short a distance of the merry old gentleman, was on his way to the bookstall. When he got into Clerkenwell he accidentally turned down a by-street which was not exactly in his way; he was startled by a young woman screaming out very loud:

'Oh, my dear brother!' And he had hardly looked up to see what the matter was, when he was stopped by having a pair of arms thrown tight round his neck.

'Don't,' cried Oliver, struggling. 'Let go of me. Who is it? What are you stopping me for?'

The only reply to this was a great number of loud lamentations from the young woman who had embraced him.

'Oh, Oliver, Oliver, you naughty boy. Come home directly, you cruel boy!'

'Why, it's Nancy!' exclaimed Oliver.

'You see, he knows me,' cried Nancy, appealing to the bystanders. 'Make him come home or he'll kill his dear mother and father.'

'What the devil's this?' said a man, bursting out of a beer-shop with a white dog at his heel. 'Young Oliver, come home to your mother, you young dog.'

They were in a dark corner, quite out of the track of passengers. Oliver saw, but too plainly, that resistance would be of no avail. He held out his hand, which Nancy clasped tight in hers, and Sikes seized the other.

They walked on by little-frequented and dirty ways, for a full half-hour. At length they turned into a filthy narrow street, nearly full of old clothes shops; the dog, running forward as if conscious that there was no further occasion for his keeping on guard, stopped before the door of a shop that was closed and apparently untenanted; the house was in ruinous condition.

'All right,' cried Sikes, glancing cautiously about.

Nancy stooped below the shutters and Oliver heard the sound of a bell. They crossed to the opposite side of the street and stood for a few moments under a lamp. A noise, as if a sash window were gently raised, was heard; and soon afterwards the door softly opened. Mr. Sikes then seized the terrified boy by the collar with very little ceremony, and all three were quickly inside the house.

The passage was perfectly dark. They waited while the person who had let them in, chained and barred the door. He brought a light and Oliver recognized Mr. John Dawkins, otherwise the Artful Dodger. He bore in his right hand a tallow candle stuck in the end of a cleft stick.

The young gentleman did not stop to bestow any other mark of recognition upon Oliver than a humorous grin, but, turning away, beckoned the visitors to follow him down a flight of stairs. They crossed an empty kitchen and, opening the door of a low earthy-smelling room, which seemed to have been built in a small back-yard, were received with a shout of laughter.

'Oh, my wig, my wig!' cried Master Charles Bates, from whose lungs the laughter had proceeded; 'here he is! Oh, cry, here he is! Oh, Fagin, look at him!'

The Jew, taking off his nightcap, made a number of low bows to the bewildered boy. The Artful, meantime, who was of a rather saturnine disposition and seldom gave way to merriment when it interfered with business, rifled Oliver's pockets with steady assiduity. Sikes seized the money and Fagin the books.

'They belong to the old gentleman,' said Oliver, wringing his hands; 'to the good, kind old gentleman who took me into his house, and had me nursed when I was near dying of the fever. Oh, pray send them back; send him back the books and money. Keep me here all my life long; but, do have mercy upon me and send them back!'

'They will think you have stolen 'em. Ha! Ha!' chuckled the Jew, rubbing his hands; 'it couldn't have happened better if we had chosen our time!'

Oliver jumped suddenly to his feet and tore wildly from the room, uttering shrieks for help which made the bare old house echo to the roof. The Jew and his two pupils darted out in pursuit and soon returned, dragging Oliver among them.

'So you wanted to get away, my dear, did you,' said the Jew taking up a jagged and knotted club which lay in a corner of the fireplace: 'eh?'

He inflicted a smart blow on Oliver's shoulders with the club, and was raising it for a second when the girl, rushing forward, wrested it from his hand. She flung it into the fire with a force that brought some of the glowing coals whirling out into the room.

'I won't stand by and see it done, Fagin,' cried the girl. 'You've got the boy, and what more would you have?— Let him be—let him be—or I shall put that mark on some of you, that will bring me to the gallows before my time.'

'Why, Nancy!' said the Jew in a soothing tone, after a pause during which he and Mr. Sikes had stared at one another in a disconcerted manner; 'you—you're more clever than ever tonight. Ha! Ha! my dear, you are acting beautifully.'

The girl made such a rush at the Jew as would probably have left signal marks of her revenge upon him, had not her wrists been seized by Sikes at the right moment; upon which she made a few ineffectual struggles, and fainted.

'She's all right now,' said Sikes, laying her down in a corner. 'She's uncommon strong in the arms when she's up in this way.'

'It's the worst of having to do with women,' said the Jew replacing his club; 'but they're clever, and we can't get on in our line without 'em. Charley, show Oliver to bed.'

Master Bates led Oliver into an adjacent kitchen, where there were two or three of the beds on which he had slept before; he produced the identical old suit of clothes which Oliver had so much congratulated himself upon leaving off at Mr. Brownlow's, and the accidental display of which to Fagin, by the Jew who had purchased them, had been the very first clue received of his whereabouts. Charley told him, amid laughter, to change.

Poor Oliver unwillingly complied. Master Bates, rolling

up the new clothes under his arm, departed from the room, leaving Oliver in the dark and locking the door behind him. Oliver, sick and weary, soon fell sound asleep.

* * * *

Now let us leave the unhappy Oliver for a while and return to the town where he was born, where we see Mr. Bumble emerging from the workhouse gate at early morning. He walked with portly carriage and commanding steps up the High Street and relaxed not in his dignified pace until he reached the farm where Mrs. Mann tended the infant paupers with parochial care.

'Mrs. Mann, ma'am, good morning,' said Mr. Bumble. 'Mrs. Mann, I am a-going to London.'

'Lauk, Mr. Bumble!' cried Mrs. Mann, starting back.

'To London, ma'am,' resumed the inflexible beadle, 'by coach—I and two paupers, Mrs. Mann! A legal action is a-coming on about a settlement; and the board has appointed me to depose to the matter before the quarter-sessions at Clerkinwell. And I very much question,' added Mr. Bumble, drawing himself up, 'whether the Clerkinwell Sessions will not find themselves in the wrong box before they have done with me.'

There was so much determination and depth of purpose about the menacing manner in which Mr. Bumble delivered himself of these words that Mrs. Mann appeared quite awed by them.

'We are forgetting business, ma'am,' said the beadle. 'Here is your porochial stipend for the month.'

Mr. Bumble produced some silver money rolled in paper and requested a receipt, which Mrs. Mann wrote. The beadle nodded blandly in acknowledgement of Mrs. Mann's curtsey, and inquired how the children were.

'They're as well as can be, the dears! Of course, except the two that died last week. And little Dick. I'll bring him to you in one minute, sir.'

After some calling Dick was discovered. The child was pale and thin; his cheeks were sunken and his eyes large and bright; his young limbs had wasted away like those of an old man. He stood trembling beneath Mr. Bumble's glance.

'I should like,' faltered the child, 'if somebody that can write, would put a few words down for me on a piece of paper, and fold it up and seal it, and keep it for me after I am laid in the ground.'

'Why, what does the boy mean?' exclaimed Mr. Bumble, on whom the earnest manner and wan aspect of the child had made some impression, accustomed as he was to such things. 'What do you mean, sir?'

'I should like,' said the child, 'to leave my dear love to poor Oliver Twist, and to let him know how often I have sat by myself and cried to think of his wandering about in the dark nights with nobody to help him.'

Mr. Bumble surveyed the little speaker from head to foot, with indescribable astonishment, and, turning to his companion, said: 'They're all in one story, Mrs. Mann. That owdacious Oliver had demogalised them all! Take him away, ma'am. This must be stated to the board, Mrs. Mann. Take him away, I can't bear the sight of him.'

Dick was immediately taken away and locked up in the coal cellar. Mr. Bumble shortly afterwards took himself off to prepare for his journey.

At six o'clock next morning, Mr. Bumble took his place on the outside of the coach, accompanied by the criminals whose settlement was disputed, with whom, in due course of time, he arrived in London.

Having disposed of these evil-minded persons for the night, Mr. Bumble sat himself down at the house at which the coach stopped and took a temperate dinner of steaks, oyster sauce and porter. Then, putting a glass of gin-and-water on the chimney-piece, he composed himself to read the paper.

The very first paragraph upon Mr. Bumble's eyes rested, was the following advertisement:

FIVE GUINEAS REWARD

'Whereas a young boy, named Oliver Twist, absconded or was enticed, on Thursday evening last, from his home at Pentonville, and has not since been heard of. The above reward will be paid to any person who will give such information as will lead to the discovery of the said Oliver Twist, or tend to throw any light upon his previous history, in which the advertiser is, for many reasons, warmly interested.'

And then followed a full description of Oliver's dress, person, appearance and disappearance, with the name and address of Mr. Brownlow at full length. In something more than five minutes Mr. Bumble was on his way to Pentonville, having actually, in his excitement, left the glass of hot gin-and-water, untasted.

He no sooner uttered Oliver's name, in explanation of his errand, than he was shown into the little back study, where Mr. Brownlow and his friend, Mr. Grimwig, sat with decanters and glasses before them. The latter gentleman at once burst into the exclamation:

'A beadle! A parish beadle, or I'll eat my head.'

'Pray don't interrupt just now,' said Mr. Brownlow. 'Take a seat, will you? Do you know where this poor boy is now?'

'No more than nobody,' replied Mr. Beadle.

'Well, what do you know of him?' inquired the gentleman. 'Speak out, my friend, if you have anything to say. What *do* you know of him?'

It would be tedious if the story was given in the beadle's words—occupying, as it did, some twenty minutes in the telling—but the sum and substance of it was: that Oliver was a foundling born of low and vicious parents; that he had, from his birth, displayed no better qualities than treachery, ingratitude and malice; that he had terminated his brief career in the place of his birth by making a sanguinary and cowardly attack on an unoffending lad, and running away in the night time from his master's house. In proof of his being the person he represented himself, Mr. Bumble laid upon the table the papers he had brought into town, then, pocketing the five guineas, he withdrew.

Mr. Brownlow paced the room to and fro for some minutes, evidently so much disturbed by the beadle's tale that even Mr. Grimwig forbore to vex him further.

At length he stopped, and rang the bell violently.

'Mrs. Bedwin,' said Mr. Brownlow, when the housekeeper appeared; 'that boy, Oliver, is an impostor.'

'It can't be, sir. It cannot be,' said the old lady energetically. 'I never will believe it, sir. Never!'

'Silence!' said the old gentleman, feigning an anger he was far from feeling. 'Never let me hear the boy's name again. I rang to tell you that. Never. Never, on any pretence, mind! You may leave the room, Mrs. Bedwin. And remember! I am in earnest.'

There were sad hearts at Mr. Brownlow's that night.

* * * *

Oliver's heart sank within him when he thought of his good kind friends; it was as well for him that he could not know what they had heard, or it might have broken outright.

About noon next day, when the Dodger and Master Bates had gone out to pursue their customary avocations, Mr. Fagin took the opportunity of reading Oliver a long lecture on the crying sin of ingratitude. He told him of another boy who had escaped and had ended his life on the gallows, and drew a rather disagreeable picture of the discomforts of hanging.

Little Oliver's blood ran cold as he listened to the Jew's words, and imperfectly comprehended the dark threats conveyed in them.

The Jew, smiling hideously, patted him on the head and said that if he kept himself quiet, and applied himself to business, he saw that they would be very good friends. Then, taking his hat, and covering himself with an old patched greatcoat, he went out and locked the room door behind him.

And so Oliver remained all that day, and for the greater part of many subsequent days, seeing nobody between early morning and midnight, and left during the long hours to commune with his own thoughts. Which, never failing to revert to his kind friends, and the opinion they must long ago have formed of him, were sad indeed.

After the lapse of a week or so, the Jew left the room door unlocked; and Oliver was at liberty to wander about the house; instructed from time to time by the Dodger as to the benefits of securing Fagin's favour without more delay, by the means which they themselves had employed to gain it.

'If you don't take pocket-handkechers and watches,' said the Dodger, reducing his conversation to the level of Oliver's capacity, 'some other cove will; so that the coves that lose 'em will be all the worse, and you'll be all the worse too, and nobody half a ha'p'orth the better, except the chaps wot gets them and you've just as good a right to them as they have.'

'To be sure, to be sure!' said the Jew, who had entered unseen by Oliver. 'It all lies in a nutshell, my dear, in a nutshell, take the Dodger's word for it. Ha! Ha! Ha! He understands the catechism of his trade.'

The conversation proceeded no farther at this time, for the Jew had returned home accompanied by Miss Betsy and a gentleman whom Oliver had never seen before but who was accosted by the Dodger as Tom Chitling, and who, having lingered on the stairs to exchange a few gallantries with the lady, now made his appearance.

Mr. Chitling was older in years than the Dodger, having perhaps numbered eighteen winters; but there was a degree of deference in his deportment towards that young gentleman which seemed to indicate that he felt himself conscious of a slight inferiority in point of genius and professional acquirements. He had small twinkling eyes and a pock-marked face, wore a fur cap, a dark corduroy jacket, greasy fustian trousers and an apron. Oliver was told he had just come out of prison.

'Where do you think the gentleman has come from, Oliver,' inquired the Jew with a grin, as the other boy put a bottle of spirits on the table.

'I—I—don't know, sir,' replied Oliver.

'He's in luck, then,' said the young man, with a meaning look at Fagin. 'Never mind where I come from, young 'un; you'll find your way there soon enough, I'll bet a crown!'

From this day Oliver was seldom left alone, but was placed in almost constant communication with the two boys, who played the old game with the Jew every day; whether for their own improvement or Oliver's, Mr. Fagin best knew. At other times the old man would tell them stories of robberies he had committed in his younger days, mixed up with so much that was droll and curious that Oliver could not help laughing heartily and showing that he was amused in spite of all his better feelings. In short, the wily old Jew had the boy in his toils. Having prepared his mind by solitude and gloom, to prefer any companionship to his own sad thoughts in such a dreary place, he was now slowly instilling into his soul the poison which he hoped would blacken it and change its hue for ever.

6

THE BURGLARY THAT FAILED

IT WAS a chill, damp, windy night, when the Jew, buttoning his greatcoat tight round his shrivelled body, and pulling the collar up over his ears so as to completely obscure the lower part of his face, emerged from his den. He stopped for an instant at the corner of the street, and glancing suspiciously around, crossed the road and struck off in the direction of Spitalfields. At the door of a house in a dismal street, he knocked; having exchanged a few muttered words with the person who opened it, he walked upstairs.

A dog growled as he touched the handle of a room door, and a man's voice demanded who was there.

'Only me, Bill; only me, my dear,' said the Jew, looking in.

'Bring in your body, then,' said Sikes.

'Ah, Nancy,' said the Jew with some embarrassment on catching sight of her for the first time since she had interfered on behalf of Oliver. 'It is cold, Nancy dear, It seems to go right through one,' added the old man, as he warmed his skinny hands over the fire.

Nancy quickly brought a bottle from a cupboard and Sikes, pouring out a glass of brandy, bade the Jew drink it off.

'Now for business,' said Sikes, 'so say what you've got to say.

'About the crib at Chertsey, Bill?' said the Jew, drawing his chair forward, and speaking in a very low voice. 'When is it to be done, eh? When is it to be done? Such plate, my dear, such plate!' said the Jew, rubbing his hands and elevating his eyebrows in a rapture of anticipation.

'Toby Crackit and me were over the garden wall the night afore last, sounding the panels of the doors and shutters. The crib's barred up at night like a jail; but there's one part we can crack, safe and softly.'

'Is there no help wanted but yours and Toby's?' asked the Jew.

'None,' said Sikes. ''Cept a centre-bit and a boy. The first we've both got; the second you must find us. I want a boy, and he mustn't be a big 'un.'

'Oliver's the boy for you, my dear,' said the Jew in a hoarse whisper. 'He's been in good training these last few weeks, and it's time he began to work for his bread. Besides, the others are all too big.'

'Well, he is just the size I want,' said Mr. Sikes, ruminating.

'And will do everything you want, Bill, my dear, that is, if you frighten him enough.'

'You'd better bring the boy here tomorrow night, then,' rejoined Sikes. 'I shall get off the stones an hour arter daybreak. Then you hold your tongue and keep the melting pot ready, and that's all you'll have to do.'

After a long discussion, in which all three took an active part, it was decided that Nancy should repair to the Jew's next evening when the night had set in, and bring Oliver away with her, Fagin craftily observing that if he evinced any disinclination to the task, he would be more willing to accompany the girl who had so recently interfered on his behalf than anybody else. It was also solemnly arranged that poor Oliver should, for the purposes of the contemplated expedition, be unreservedly consigned to the care and custody of Mr. William Sikes.

Mr. Fagin wended his way, through mud and mire, to his gloomy abode, where the Dodger was sitting up, impatiently awaiting his return.

'Is Oliver a-bed? I want to speak to him,' was his first remark as they descended the stairs.

'Hours ago!' replied the Dodger, throwing open a door. 'Here he is!'

'Not now,' said the Jew, turning softly away. 'Tomorrow. Tomorrow.'

When Oliver awoke in the morning, he was a good deal surprised to find that a new pair of shoes, with strong, thick soles, had been placed at his bedside, and that his old shoes had been removed. The Jew told him, in a tone and manner, which increased his alarm, that he was to be taken to the residence of Bill Sikes that night.

'To—to—stop there, sir?' asked Oliver anxiously.

'No, no, my dear. Not to stop there,' replied the Jew. 'We shouldn't like to lose you. Don't be afraid, Oliver, you shall come back to us again.

After this, the Jew remained very surly and silent till night, when he prepared to go abroad. Then, gazing fixed at the boy, he shook his right hand before him in a warning manner.

'Take heed, Oliver! Take heed!' he threatened. 'Sikes is a rough man and thinks nothing of blood when his own is up. Whatever falls out, say nothing; and do what he bids you. Mind!'

Oliver was pondering, with trembling heart, on the Jew's words, when a rustling noise aroused him. It was Nancy.

'I have come from Bill,' explained the girl. 'You are to go with me. Give me your hand. Make haste! Your hand!'

A hackney-cabriolet was in waiting; the girl pulled Oliver in with her and pulled the curtains close. The driver wanted no directions, but lashed his horse into full speed, without the delay of an instant.

The carriage stopped at the house to which the Jew's steps had been directed on the previous evening. They went quickly inside.

'This way,' said the girl, releasing her hold for the first time.

'Hullo!' replied Sikes, appearing at the head of the stairs. 'So you've got the kid. Come here, young 'un, and let me read you a lectur', which is as well got over at once. Now first: do you know wot this is?' inquired Sikes, taking up a pocket pistol which lay on the table.

Oliver replied in the affirmative.

'Well, then, look here,' continued Sikes. 'This is powder; that 'ere's a bullet; and this is a little bit of a old hat for waddin'. Now it's loaded,' said Mr. Sikes when he had finished. 'Well,' said the robber, grasping Oliver's wrist, and putting the barrel so close to his temple that it touched— at which moment the boy could not repress a start—'if you speak a word when you're out o'doors with me, except when I speak to you, that loading will be in your head without notice. So, if you *do* make up your mind to speak without leave, say your prayers first.'

Having bestowed a scowl upon the object of this warning, to increase its effect, Mr. Sikes continued: 'And now that he's thoroughly up to it, let's have some supper, and get a snooze before starting.'

Supper being ended—it may easily be conceived that Oliver had no great appetite for it—Mr. Sikes disposed of a couple of glasses of spirits and water, threw himself on the bed, ordering Nancy with many imprecations in case of failure, to call him at five precisely. Oliver stretched himself in his clothes, by command of the same authority, on a mattress on the floor, and weary with anxiety, he at length fell asleep.

'Now, then,' growled Sikes next morning, 'half-past five! Look sharp, or you'll get no breakfast, for it's late as it is.'

Nancy, scarcely looking at the boy, threw him a hand-kerchief to tie round his throat; Sikes gave him a large, rough cape to button over his shoulders. Thus attired, he gave his hand to the robber, who, merely pausing to show him with a menacing gesture that he had that same pistol in a side pocket of his greatcoat, clasped it firmly in his, and, exchanging a farewell with Nancy, led him away.

It was a cheerless morning when they got into the street; blowing, and raining hard, and the clouds looking dull and stormy.

By the time they had turned into the Bethnal Green road, the day had fairly begun to break. As they approached the city the noise and traffic gradually 'increased; when they threaded the streets between Shoreditch and Smithfield, it had swelled to a roar of sound and bustle.

Turning down Sun Street and Crown Street, and crossing Finsbury Square, Mr. Sikes struck, by way of Chiswell Street into Barbican: thence into Long Lane, and so into Smithfield, from which latter place arose a tumult of discordant sounds that filled Oliver Twist with amazement.

Mr. Sikes, dragging Oliver after him, elbowed his way through the thickest of the crowd, until they were clear of the turmoil and had made their way through Hosier lane into Holborn.

'Now, young 'un!' said Sikes, looking up at the clock of

St. Andrew's Church, 'hard upon seven! You must step out. Come, don't lag behind already, Lazy-legs!'

They held their course at this rate until they had passed Hyde Park Corner and were on their way to Kensington, when Sikes relaxed his pace until an empty cart which was at some little distance behind, came up. Seeing 'Hounslow' written on it, he asked the driver with as much civility as he could assume, if he would give them a lift as far as Isleworth.

'Jump up,' said the man. 'Is that your boy?'

'Yes; he's my boy,' said Sikes, looking hard at Oliver, and putting his hand abstractedly into the pocket where the pistol was.

As they passed the different milestones Oliver wondered more and more, where his companion meant to take him. Kensington, Hammersmith, Chiswick, New Bridge, Brentford, were all passed; and yet they went on as steadily as if they had only just begun their journey. At length they came to a public-house called the Coach and Horses, a little way beyond which another road appeared to turn off. And here the cart stopped.

Sikes dismounted with great precipitation, holding Oliver by the hand all the while, and lifting him down directly, bestowed a furious look upon him and rapped the side pocket with his fist in a significant manner; then, telling Oliver he might look about him if he wanted, once again led him onward on his journey, passing many large gardens and gentlemen's houses on both sides of the way, and stopping for nothing but a little beer until they reached a town. Here, against the wall of a house, Oliver saw written up in pretty large letters 'Hampton'. They lingered about in the fields for some hours. At length they came back into the town and, turning into an old public house with a defaced signboard, ordered some dinner by the kitchen fire. After the meal, being much tired with the walk and getting up so early, Oliver dozed a little at first; then quite overpowered by fatigue and the fumes of tobacco, fell asleep.

It was quite dark when he was awakened by a push from Sikes. Rousing himself sufficiently to sit up and look about him, he found that worthy in close fellowship and communication with a labouring man, over a pint of ale.

'So, you're going on to Lower Halliford, are you?' inquired Sikes.

'Yes, I am,' replied the man, who seemed a little the worse —or better, as the case might be—for drinking.

'Could you give my boy and me a lift as far as there?' demanded Sikes, pushing the ale towards his new friend.

'If you're going directly, I can,' replied the man, looking out of the pot. 'Are you going to Halliford?'

'Going on to Shepperton,' replied Sikes.

'I'm your man as far as I go,' replied the other.

After the exchange of a few compliments, they bade the company good night and went out, into the dark night.

Oliver sat huddled together in a corner of the cart, bewildered with alarm and apprehension, and figuring strange objects in the gaunt trees, whose branches waved grimly to and fro as if in some fantastic joy at the desolation of the scene.

Sunbury was passed through as the church clock struck seven, and they came again into the lonely road. Two or three miles more, and the cart stopped. Sikes alighted, took Oliver by the hand, and they once again walked on.

They turned into no house at Shepperton, as the weary boy had expected, but still kept walking on, in mud and darkness, through gloomy lanes and over cold open wastes, until they came within sight of the lights of a town at no great distance. On looking intently forward, Oliver saw that the water was just below them, and that they were coming to the foot of a bridge. He saw that they stood before a solitary house, all ruinous, decayed. The house was dark, dismantled, and to all appearance, uninhabited.

Sikes, with Oliver's hand still in his, softly approached the low porch and raised the latch. The door yielded to the pressure and they passed in together.

'Hallo!' cried a hoarse voice, as soon as they set foot in the passage.

'Don't make such a row,' said Sikes, bolting the door. 'Show a glim, Toby.'

'Aha, my pal!' cried the same voice. 'A glim, Barney, a glim! Show the gentleman in, Barney.'

Next appeared the form of the same individual who has been

heretofore described as labouring under the infirmity of speaking through his nose, and officiating as waiter at the public house on Saffron Hill.

'Bister Sikes!' exclaimed Barney, with real or counterfeit joy; 'cub id, sir, cub id.'

Sikes pushed Oliver before him; and they entered a low, dark room with a smoky fire, two or three broken chairs, a table and a very old couch, on which, with his legs much higher than his head, a man was reposing at full length smoking a long clay pipe. Mr. Toby Crackit (for he it was) rested his eye upon Oliver, brought himself into a sitting posture, and demanded who that was.

'The boy. Only the boy!' replied Sikes, drawing a chair towards the fire.

'Wud of Bister Fagid's lads,' exclaimed Barney, with a grin.

Sikes having satisfied his appetite (Oliver could eat nothing but a small crust of bread which they made him swallow), Barney stretched himself on the floor in a blanket, the two men laid themselves down on chairs for a short nap, and Oliver fell into a heavy doze from which he was roused by Toby Crackit jumping up and declaring it was half-past one.

In an instant the other two were on their legs, and all were actively engaged in busy preparation. Sikes and his companion enveloped their necks and chins in large dark shawls, and drew on their greatcoats; Barney, opening a cupboard, brought forth several articles which he hastily crammed into the pockets.

'Barkers for me, Barney,' said Toby Crackit.

'Here they are,' replied Barney, producing a pair of pistols; 'you loaded them yourself.'

'All right,' replied Toby, stowing them away. 'The persuaders?'

'I've got 'em,' replied Sikes.

'Crape, keys, centre-bits, darkies—nothing forgotten?' inquired Toby, fastening a small crowbar to a loop inside the skirt of his coat.

'All right,' replied his companion, 'bring them bits of timber, Barney. That's the time of day.'

With these words he took a thick stick from Barney's hands, who, having delivered another to Toby, busied himself in fastening on Oliver's cape.

'Now then!' said Sikes, holding out his hand.

Oliver, who was completely stupefied by the unwonted exercise and the air and the drink which had been forced upon him, put his hand mechanically into that which Sikes extended for the purpose.

'Take his other hand, Toby.' said Sikes.

The two robbers issued forth with Oliver between them. Barney, having made all fast, rolled himself up as before, and was soon asleep again.

It was now intensely dark and much foggier. They crossed the bridge and kept on towards the lights which Oliver had seen before. They were at no great distance off; and as they walked pretty briskly, they soon arrived at Chertsey.

'Slap through the town,' whispered Sikes, 'there'll be nobody in the way tonight to see us.'

They had cleared the town as the church bell struck two.

Quickening their pace, they turned up a road upon the left hand. After walking about a quarter of a mile, they stopped before a detached house, surrounded by a wall, to the top of which, Toby Crackit, scarcely pausing to take breath, climbed in a twinkling. Sikes hoisted Oliver up and followed directly; and they stole cautiously towards the house.

And now, for the first time, Oliver, well-nigh mad with grief and terror, saw that housebreaking and robbery, if not murder, were the objects of the expedition. But his protests were answered by threats. A mist came before his eyes, the cold sweat stood upon his ashy face; his limbs failed him; and he sank upon his knees. Toby placed his hand upon the boy's mouth and dragged him to the house.

'Here, Bill,' cried Toby, 'wrench the shutter open. He's game enough now, I'll engage. I've seen older hands of his age took the same way, for a minute or two on a cold night.'

Sikes, invoking terrific imprecations upon Fagin's head for sending Oliver on such an errand, plied the crowbar vigorously, but with little noise. After some delay, and some assistance from Toby, the shutter to which he had referred, swung open on its hinges.

It was a little lattice window, about five feet and a half above the ground, at the back of the house, which belonged to a scullery, or small brewing place, at the end of the passage. A very brief exercise of Mr. Sikes's art sufficed to overcome the fastening of the lattice, and it soon stood wide open also.

'Now listen, you young limb,' whispered Sikes, drawing a dark lantern from his pocket and throwing the glare full on Oliver's face: 'I'm a-goin' to put you through there. Take this light, go softly up the steps straight afore you, and along the little hall to the street door; unfasten it and let us in.'

'Take this lantern,' said Sikes, looking into the room. 'You see the stairs afore you?'

Oliver, more dead than alive, gasped out, 'Yes.' Sikes, pointing to the street door with the pistol barrel, briefly advised him to take notice that he was within shot all the way, and if he faltered, he would be dead that instant.

In the short time that he had had to collect his senses, the boy had firmly resolved that, whether he died in the attempt or not, he would make one effort to dart upstairs from the hall and alarm the family. Filled with this idea, he advanced at once, but stealthily.

'Come back!' suddenly cried Sikes aloud. 'Back! Back!'

Startled, Oliver let his lantern fall, and knew not whether to advance or fly.

A light appeared—a vision of two terrified half-dressed men at the top of the stairs swam before his eyes—a flash—a loud noise—a smoke—a crash somewhere, but where he knew not—and he staggered back.

Sikes fired his own pistol after the men, who were already retreating, and dragged the boy up.

'Clasp your arm tighter,' said Sikes, as he drew him through the window. 'Give me a shawl here. They've hit him. Quick! How the boy bleeds!'

Then came the loud ringing of a bell, mingled with the noise of fire-arms, and the shouts of men, and the sensation of being carried over uneven ground at a rapid pace. And then the noises grew confused in the distance, and a cold, deadly feeling crept over the boy's heart; and he saw, or heard, no more.

7

A BEADLE IN LOVE AND A THIEF IN A TEMPER

THE night was bitterly cold. The snow lay on the ground frozen into a thick hard crust, when Mrs. Corney, the matron of the workhouse where Oliver Twist was born, sat herself down before a cheerful fire in her own little room, and was about to solace herself with a cup of tea. She had just tasted the first cup when she was disturbed by a soft tap at the room door.

'Oh, come in with you!' said Mrs. Corney sharply. 'Sòme of the old women dying, I suppose. They always die when I'm at meals. Don't stand there letting the cold air in, don't. What's amiss now, eh?'

'Nothing, ma'am, nothing,' replied a man's voice.

'Dear me!' exclaimed the matron, in a much sweeter tone. 'Is that Mr. Bumble?'

'At your service, ma'am.'

'Hard weather, Mr. Bumble,' said the matron.

'Hard, indeed, ma'am,' replied the beadle. 'Anti-porochial weather, this, ma'am.'

The matron looked from the little kettle to the beadle, and bashfully inquired whether—whether he wouldn't take a cup of tea?

Mr. Bumble instantaneously drew another chair up to the table. As he slowly seated himself, he looked at the lady. She fixed her eyes upon the little teapot. Mr. Bumble coughed again, and slightly smiled.

Mrs. Corney rose to get another cup and saucer from the closet. As she sat down again, her eyes once more encountered those of the gallant beadle; she coloured, and applied herself to the task of making his tea. Again Mr. Bumble coughed—louder this time than he had coughed yet.

'Sweet, Mr. Bumble?' inquired the matron, taking up the sugar basin.

'Very sweet indeed, ma'am,' replied Mr. Bumble. He fixed his eyes on Mrs. Corney as he said this; and if ever a beadle looked tender, Mr. Bumble was that beadle at the moment.

'You have a cat, ma'am, I see,' said Mr. Bumble. 'Any cat or kitten, that could live with you, ma'am, and not be fond of its home, must be a ass, ma'am.'

'Oh, Mr. Bumble!' remonstrated Mrs. Corney.

'It's of no use disguising the facts, ma'am,' said Mr. Bumble, slowly flourishing the teaspoon with a kind of amorous dignity which made him doubly impressive; 'I would drown it myself, with pleasure.'

'Then you're a cruel man,' said the matron vivaciously, as she held out her hand for the beadle's cup, 'and a very hard-hearted man besides.'

'Hard-hearted, ma'am?' said Mr. Bumble. 'Hard?' Mr. Bumble resigned his cup without another word, squeezed Mrs. Corney's little finger as she took it, and inflicting two open-handed slaps upon his laced waistcoat, gave a mighty sigh and hitched his chair a very little morsel farther from the fire.

It was a round table, consequently Mr. Bumble, by moving his chair by little and little, soon began to diminish the distance between himself and the matron, and, continuing to travel round the outer edge of the circle, brought his chair, in time, close to that in which the matron was seated. Indeed, the two chairs touched; and when they did so, Mr. Bumble stopped.

Now, the matron remained where she was, and handed Mr. Bumble another cup of tea.

'Hard-hearted, Mrs. Corney?' said Mr. Bumble stirring his tea, and looking up into the matron's face. 'Are you hard-hearted, Mrs. Corney?'

'Dear me!' exclaimed the matron, 'what a very curious question from a single man. What can you want to know for, Mr. Bumble?'

The beadle drank his tea to the last drop, finished a piece of toast, whisked the crumbs off his knees, wiped his lips, and deliberately kissed the matron.

'Mr. Bumble!' cried that discreet lady. 'Mr. Bumble, I shall scream!' Mr. Bumble made no reply, but in a slow and dignified manner, put his arm round the matron's waist.

As the lady had stated her intention of screaming, of course she would have screamed at this additional boldness, but that the exertion was rendered unnecessary by a hasty knocking at the door. As Mr. Bumble darted with much agility from his seat, the matron sharply demanded who was there.

'If you please, mistress,' said a withered old female pauper, hideously ugly, putting her head in at the door, 'old Sally is a-going fast but she's troubled in her mind; she says she has got something to tell, which you must hear. She'll never die quiet till you come, mistress.'

At this intelligence, the worthy Mrs. Corney muttered a variety of invectives and muffling herself in a thick shawl which she hastily caught up, briefly requested Mr. Bumble to stay until she came back, lest anything particular should occur.

Mr. Bumble, on being left to himself examined the silver and then seemed to be mentally engaged in taking an exact inventory of the furniture.

Meanwhile the old crone tottered along the passages and up the stairs, muttering some indistinct answers to the chidings of her companion; being at length compelled to pause for breath, she gave the light into her hand and remained behind to follow as she might, while the more nimble superior made her way to the room where the sick woman lay.

It was a bare garret-room, with a dim light burning at the farther end. There was another old woman watching by the bed; the parish apothecary's apprentice was standing by the fire making a toothpick out of a quill.

'Oh!' said the young man, turning his face towards the bed, 'it's all U.P. there, Mrs. Corney. If she lasts a couple of hours I shall be surprised.' Then he planted himself in front of the fire and made good use of it for ten minutes or so, when apparently growing rather dull, he wished Mrs. Corney joy of her job, and took himself off on tiptoe.

When they had sat in silence for some time, the two old women rose from the bed and crouching over the fire, held out their withered hands to catch the heat. The flame threw a ghastly light on their shrivelled faces, and made their ugliness appear terrible, as, in this position, they began to converse in a low voice.

'Did she say any more, Anny dear, while I was gone?' inquired the messenger.

'Not a word,' replied the other old crone. 'She plucked and tore at her arms for a little time; but I held her hands and she soon dropped off. She hasn't much strength in her, so I easily kept her quiet.'

A cry from the two women, who had turned towards the bed, caused the matron to look round. The patient had raised herself upright and was stretching her arms towards them.

'Who's that?' she cried in a hollow voice.

'Hush, hush!' said one of the women, stooping over her. 'Lie down, lie down!'

'I'll never lie down again alive,' said the woman, struggling. 'I *will* tell her! Come here! Nearer! Let me whisper in your ear!'

She clutched the matron by the arm and forcing her into a chair by the bedside, was about to speak, when looking round, she caught sight of the two old women bending forward in the attitude of eager listeners.

'Turn them away!' said the woman drowsily. 'Make haste! Make haste!'

The superior pushed them from the room, closed the door, and returned to the bedside.

'Now listen to me,' said the dying woman aloud, as if making a great effort to revive one latent spark of energy. 'In this very room—in this very bed—I once nursed a pretty young creetur' that was brought into the house with her feet cut and bruised from walking, and all soiled with dust and blood. She gave birth to a boy and died. Let me think—what was the year again?'

'Never mind the year,' said the impatient auditor; 'what about her?'

'Ay,' murmured the sick woman, relapsing into her former drowsy state, 'what about her?—What about—I know!' she cried, jumping fiercely up, her face flushed and her eyes starting from her head. . . . 'I robbed her, so I did! She wasn't cold—I tell you she wasn't cold, when I stole it!'

'Stole what, for God's sake?' cried the matron, with a gesture as if she would call for help.

'It,' replied the woman, laying her hand over the other's mouth. 'The only thing she had. She wanted clothes to keep her warm, and food to eat; but she had kept it safe, and had it in her bosom. It was gold, I tell you! Rich gold, that might have saved her life!'

'Gold!' echoed the matron, bending eagerly over the woman as she fell back. 'Go on, go on—yes—what of it? Who was the mother? When was it?'

'She charged me to keep it safe,' replied the woman with a groan, 'and trusted me as the only woman about her. I stole it in my heart when she first showed it me hanging round her neck; and the child's death, perhaps, is on me besides! They would have treated him better if they had known it all!'

'Known what?' asked the other. 'Speak!'

'The boy grew so like his mother,' said the woman, rambling on and not heeding the question, 'that I could never forget it when I saw his face.'

'The boy's name?' demanded the matron.

'They *called* him Oliver,' replied the woman feebly. 'The gold I stole was——'

'Yes, yes—hat?' cried the other.

She was bending eagerly over the other to hear her reply, but drew back instinctively, as she once again rose, slowly and stiffly, into a sitting posture, then, clutching the coverlid with both hands, muttered some indistinct sounds in her throat, and fell lifeless on the bed.

* * * *

While these things were passing in the county workhouse, Mr. Fagin sat in the old den—the same from which Oliver had been removed by the girl—brooding over a dull, smoky fire.

At a table behind him sat the Artful Dodger, Master Charley Bates and Mr. Chitling, all intent upon a game of whist.

'Hark!' cried the Dodger at this moment, 'I heard the tinkler.' Catching up the light he crept softly upstairs.

The bell was rung again, with some impatience, while the party were in darkness. After a short pause, the Dodger re-appeared, followed by a man in a coarse smock-frock, Toby Crackit, all haggard, unwashed, and unshorn.

'How are you, Fagey?' said this worthy, nodding to the Jew. Then ordering the others out, he closed the door, mixed a glass of spirits and water, and composed himself for talking.

'First and foremost, Fagey,' said the housebreaker, 'how's Bill?'

'What?' screamed the Jew, starting from his seat.

'Why, you don't mean to say——' began Toby, turning pale.

'Mean!' cried the Jew, stamping furiously on the ground. 'Where are they? Sikes and the boy! Where are they? Where have they been? Where are they hiding? Why have they not been here?'

'The crack failed,' said Toby faintly.

'I know it,' replied the Jew, tearing a newspaper from his pocket and pointing to it. 'What more?'

'They fired and hit the boy. We cut over the fields at the back with him between us—straight as the crow flies—through hedge and ditch. They gave chase. Damme! The whole country was awake, and the dogs upon us.'

'The boy!'

'Bill had him on his back and scudded like the wind. We stopped to take him between us; his head hung down and he was cold. They were close upon our heels; every man for himself and each from the gallows! We parted company and left the youngster lying in a ditch. Alive or dead, that's all I know about him.'

The Jew stopped to hear no more, but uttering a loud yell, and twining his hands in his hair, rushed from the room, and from the house.

Skulking only through the by-ways and alleys, he at length emerged near to the spot on which Snow Hill and Holborn Hill meet, where there opens upon the right hand as you come out of the City, a narrow and dismal alley leading to Saffron Hill. It was to a public house in this vile alley that the Jew hastened.

The Three Cripples, or rather the Cripples, which was the sign by which the establishment was familiarly known to its patrons, was the public house in which Mr. Sikes and his dog have already figured. Merely making a sign to a man at the bar, Fagin walked straight upstairs, and opening the door of a room and softly insinuating himself into the chamber, looked anxiously about, shading his eyes with his hand as if in search of some particular person.

The room was illuminated by two gaslights, the glare of which was prevented by the barred shutters and closely drawn curtains of faded red, from being visible outside. An assemblage of heads, as confused as the noises that greeted the ear, might be made out, crowded round a long table at the upper end of which sat a chairman with a hammer of office in his hand.

Fagin, succeeding at length in catching the eye of the man who occupied the chair, beckoned to him slightly and left the room as quietly as he had entered it.

'What can I do for you, Mr. Fagin?' inquired the man, as he followed him out to the landing.

'Is he here?' asked the Jew in a whisper.

'No,' replied the man.

'And no news of Barney?' inquired Fagin.

'None,' replied the landlord of the Cripples, for it was he. 'He won't stir till it's all safe. Depend on it, they're on the scent down there; and that if he moved, he'd blow upon the thing at once. He's all right enough, Barney is, else I should have heard of him.

'Will *he* be here tonight?' asked the Jew, laying the same emphasis on the pronoun as before.

'Monks, do you mean?' inquired the landlord, hesitating.

'Hush!' said the Jew, 'yes.'

'Certain,' replied the man, drawing a gold watch from his fob. 'I expected him here before now. If you'll wait ten minutes, he'll be——'

'No, no,' said the Jew, hastily. 'Tell him that I came here to see him and that he must come to see me tonight. No, say tomorrow. As he is not here tomorrow will be time enough.'

'Good,' said the man; 'nothing more?'

'Not a word now,' said the Jew descending the stairs.

He was no sooner alone than his countenance resumed its former expression of anxiety and thought. After a brief reflection he called a hack cabriolet and bade the man drive towards Bethnal Green. He dismissed him within some quarter of a mile of Mr. Sikes's residence, and performed the short remainder of the distance on foot.

'Now,' muttered the Jew, as he knocked at the door, 'if there is any deep play here, I shall have it out of you, Nancy, my girl, cunning as you are.'

She was in her room, the woman said. Fagin crept softly upstairs, and entered it without any previous ceremony. The girl was alone, lying with her head upon the table and her hair straggling over it.

The old man turned to close the door and the noise thus occasioned roused the girl. She eyed his crafty face narrowly as she inquired whether there was any news, and as she listened to his recital of Toby Crackit's story. When it was concluded she sank into her former attitude, but spoke not a word, while the Jew looked restlessly about the room as if to assure himself that there was no appearance of Sikes having covertly returned.

Having accomplished his twofold object of imparting to the girl what he had that night heard, and of ascertaining, with his own eyes, that Sikes had not returned, Mr. Fagin again turned his face homeward.

It was within an hour of midnight. The weather being dark, and piercing cold, he had no great temptation to loiter. He had reached the corner of his own street, and was already fumbling in his pocket for the doorkey, when a dark figure emerged from a projecting entrance which lay in deep shadow, and crossing the road, glided up to him unperceived.

'Fagin!' whispered a voice close to his ear.

'Ah!' said the Jew, turning quickly round, 'is that——'

'Yes!' interrupted the stranger, 'I have been lingering here these two hours. Where the devil have you been?'

'On your business, my dear,' replied the Jew, glancing uneasily at his companion and slackening his pace as he spoke. 'On your business all night.'

At the house Fagin unlocked the door and beckoning the man to follow him, he led the way upstairs.

They conversed for some time in whispers. Though nothing of the conversation was distinguishable beyond a few disjointed words here and there, a listener might easily have perceived that Fagin appeared to be defending himself against some remarks of the stranger, and that the latter was in a state of considerable irritation. They might have been talking thus for a quarter of an hour or more when Monks—by which name the Jew had designated the strange man several times in the course of their colloquy—said, raising his voice a little:

'I tell you again, it was badly planned. Why not have kept him here among the rest, and made a sneaking, snivelling pickpocket of him at once? If you had had patience for a twelvemonth, at most, couldn't you have got him convicted and sent safely out of the kingdom, perhaps for life?'

'Who's turn would that have served, my dear?' inquired the Jew humbly.

'Mine,' replied Monks.

'But not mine,' said the Jew submissively. 'I saw it was not easy to train him to the business. He was not like other boys in the same circumstances.'

'Curse him, no,' muttered the man, 'or he would have been a thief long ago.'

'You want him made a thief. If he is alive I can make him one from this time; and if—if——' said the Jew, drawing nearer to the other—'it's not likely, mind—but if the worst comes to the worst, and he is dead——'

'It's no fault of mine if he is!' interposed the other man with a look of terror and clasping the Jew's arm with trembling hands. 'Mind that, Fagin! I had no hand in it. Anything but his death, I told you from the first. I won't shed blood; it's always found out, and haunts a man besides. If they shot him dead, I was not the cause; do you hear me? Fire this infernal den! What's that?'

'What!' cried the Jew, grasping the coward round the body with both arms as he sprang to his feet. 'Where?'

'Yonder!' replied the man, glaring at the opposite wall. 'The shadow! I saw the shadow of a woman, in a cloak and bonnet, pass along the wainscot like a breath!'

They rushed tumultuously from the room. The candle showed them only the empty staircase and their own white faces.

'It's your fancy,' said the Jew, taking up the light and turning to his companion.

'I'll swear I saw it!' replied Monks, trembling. 'It was bending forward when I saw it first; and when I spoke it darted away.'

Fagin took him into all the rooms. They were cold, bare and empty. Mr. Monks's protestations gradually became less and less and he at last confessed it could only have been his excited imagination. He declined any renewal of the conversation, however, for that night, suddenly remembering that it was past one o'clock. And so the amiable couple parted.

* * * *

Mr. Bumble was still placidly surveying the matron's room when its owner, hurrying into the room, threw herself in a breathless state on a chair by the fireside, and covering her eyes with one hand, placed the other over her heart and gasped for breath.

'Mrs. Corney,' said Mr. Bumble, stooping over the matron. 'What is this, ma'am? Has anything happened, ma'am? Pray answer me; I'm on—on——' Mr. Bumble in his alarm could not immediately think of the word 'tenterhooks', so he said 'broken bottles'.

'Oh, Mr. Bumble!' cried the lady, 'I've been so dreadfully put out!'

Mr. Bumble drew a chair beside the matron and tenderly inquired what had happened to distress her.

'Nothing,' replied Mrs. Corney. 'I am a foolish, excitable, weak creetur.'

'Not weak, ma'am,' retorted Mr. Bumble, drawing his chair a little closer. 'Are you a weak creetur, Mrs. Corney?'

'We are all weak creeturs,' said Mrs. Corney, laying down a general principle.

'So we are,' said the beadle.

Nothing was said on either side, for a minute or two afterwards. By the expiration of that time, Mr. Bumble had illustrated the position by removing his left arm from the back of Mrs. Corney's chair, where it had previously rested, to Mrs. Corney's apron string, round which it gradually became entwined.

'We are all weak creeturs,' said Mr. Bumble.

Mrs. Corney sighed.

'Don't sigh, Mrs. Corney,' said Mr. Bumble.

'I can't help it,' said Mrs. Corney, and she sighed again.

'This is a very comfortable room, ma'am,' said Mr. Bumble, looking round. 'Another room, ma'am, and this would be a complete thing.'

'It would be too much for one,' murmured the lady.

'But not for two, ma'am,' rejoined Mr. Bumble, in soft accents. 'Eh, Mrs. Corney? You know that Mr. Slout is worse tonight, my fascinator?'

'Yes,' replied Mrs. Corney bashfully.

'He can't live a week, the doctor says,' pursued Mr. Bumble. 'He is the master of this establishment; his death will cause a wacancy: that wacancy must be filled up. Oh, Mrs. Corney, what a prospect this opens! What a opportunity for jining hearts and housekeepings!'

Mrs. Corney sobbed.

'The little word?' said Mr. Bumble, bending over the bashful beauty. 'The one little, little, little word, my blessed Corney?'

'Ye—ye—yes!' sighed out the matron.

'One more,' pursed the beadle; 'compose your darling feelings for only one more. When is it to come off?'

Mrs. Corney twice essayed to speak and twice failed. At length summoning up courage, she threw her arms around Mr. Bumble's neck, and said it might be as soon as ever he pleased, and that he was 'a irresistible duck'.

Matters being thus amicably and satisfactorily arranged, the contract was solemnly ratified in teacupful of the peppermint mixture, which was rendered the more necessary by the flutter and agitation of the lady's spirits. While it was being disposed of she acquainted Mr. Bumble with the old woman's decease.

'Very good,' said that gentleman, sipping his peppermint. 'I'll call at Sowerberry's as I go home, and tell him to send tomorrow morning.'

Mr. Bumble left the building with a light heart and bright visions of his future promotion, which served to occupy his mind until he reached the shop of the undertaker.

Now, Mr. and Mrs. Sowerberry having gone out to tea and

supper, and Noah Claypole not being at any time disposed to take upon himself a greater amount of physical exertion than is necessary to a convenient performance of the two functions of eating and drinking, the shop was not closed although it was past the usual hour of shutting-up. Mr. Bumble tapped on the counter with his cane several times; but attracting no attention and beholding a light shining through the glass window of the little parlour at the back of the shop, he went through to the back of the shop and found Noah Claypole kissing Charlotte.

'What!' cried Mr. Bumble, bursting into the room. 'Do that again, sir.'

Charlotte uttered a scream and hid her face in her apron, Mr. Claypole gazed at the beadle in drunken terror.

'Do it again, you wile, owdacious fellow!' said Mr. Bumble. 'And how dare you encourage him, you insolent minx? Kiss her!' exclaimed Mr. Bumble in strong indignation, 'Faugh!'

'I didn't mean to do it,' said Noah blubbering. 'She's always a-kissing of me, whether I like it or not.'

'Oh, Noah,' cried Charlotte reproachfully.

'Silence!' said Mr. Bumble, sternly. 'Take yourself downstairs, ma'am. Noah, you shut up the shop. Tell your master that Mr. Bumble said he was to send an old woman's shell after breakfast tomorrow morning. Do you hear, sir? Kissing!' cried Mr. Bumble holding up his hands. 'The sin and wickedness of the lower orders in this porochial district is frightful!'

8

OLIVER AMONG FRIENDS

'WOLVES tear your throats!' muttered Sikes, grinding his teeth. 'I wish I was among some of you; you'd howl the hoarser for it.'

Sikes rested the body of the wounded boy across his bended knee, and turned his head for an instant to look at his pursuers. There was little to be made out, in the mist and darkness; but the loud shouting of men vibrated through the air, and the barking of the neighbouring dogs, roused by the sound of the alarm bell, resounded in every direction. Sikes laid the boy in a dry ditch at his feet, and drew a pistol from his pocket.

At this moment the noise grew louder. Sikes, again looking round could discern that the men who had given chase were already climbing the gate of the field in which he stood; and that a couple of dogs were some paces in advance of them.

'It's all up, Bill!' cried Toby. 'Drop the kid and show 'em your heels.' With this parting advice, Mr. Crackit preferring the chance of being shot by his friend to the certainty of being taken by his enemies, fairly turned tail and darted off at full speed. Sikes clenched his teeth, took one look around, threw over the prostrate form of Oliver the cape in which he had been hurriedly muffled, cleared the hedge at a bound, and was gone.

'Ho, ho, there!' cried a tremulous voice in the rear. 'Pincher, Neptune, come here, come here!'

The dogs, who in common with their masters seemed to have no particular relish for the sport in which they were engaged, readily answered to the command.

'My advice, or leastways, I should say, my *orders* is,' said the fattest man of the party, 'that we 'mediately go home again.'

'I am agreeable to anything which is agreeable to Mr. Giles,' said a shorter man, who was by no means of a slim figure, and who was very pale in the face and very polite, as frightened men frequently are.

'I shouldn't wish to appear ill-mannered, gentlemen,' said the third who had called the dogs back. 'Mr. Giles ought to know.'

This dialogue was held between the two men who had surprised the burglars, and a travelling tinker who had been sleeping in an outhouse, and who had been roused, together with his two mongrel curs, to join in the pursuit. Mr. Giles acted in the double capacity of butler and steward to the old lady of the mansion; Brittles was a lad of all-work who, having entered her service a mere child, was treated as a promising young boy still, though he was something past thirty. They hastened back to the house.

Oliver lay motionless and insensible on the spot where Sikes had left him.

Morning drew on apace. The rain came down thick and fast, and pattered noisily among the leafless bushes. At length a low cry of pain broke the stillness that prevailed; and uttering it the boy awoke. His left arm, rudely bandaged in a shawl, hung heavy and useless at his side; the bandage was saturated with blood. He was so weak that he could scarcely raise himself into a sitting posture; when he had done so, he looked feebly round for help and groaned with pain. Trembling in every joint with cold and exhaustion, he made an effort to stand upright but, shuddering from head to foot, fell prostrate on the ground.

After a short return of the stupor in which he had been so long plunged, Oliver—urged by a creeping sickness at his heart, which seemed to warn him that if he lay there he must surely die—got upon his feet and essayed to walk. His head was dizzy, and he staggered to and fro like a drunken man. Thus he staggered on, creeping, almost mechanically, between the bars of gates, or through hedge gaps as they came in his way, until he reached a road. Here the rain began to fall so heavily that it roused him.

He looked about and saw that at no great distance there was a house, which perhaps he could reach. He summoned up all his strength for one last trial, and bent his faltering steps towards it.

As he drew nearer to this house, a feeling came over him that he had seen it before. He remembered nothing of its details but the shape and aspect of the building seemed familiar to him. That garden wall! It was the very house they had attempted to rob.

Oliver pushed against the garden gate; it was unlocked and swung open on its hinges. He tottered across the lawn, climbed the steps, knocked faintly at the door, and, his whole strength failing him, sunk down against one of the pillars of the little portico.

It happened that about this time, Mr. Giles, Brittles, and the tinker were recruiting themselves after the fatigues and terrors of the night with tea and sundries in the kitchen. Not that it was Mr. Giles's habit to admit to too great familiarity the humbler servants, but death, fires, and burglary made all men equals; so Mr. Giles gave a circumstantial and minute account of the robbery, to which his hearers (but especially the cook and housemaid, who were of the party) listened with breathless interest.

Mr. Giles had risen from his seat and taken two steps with his eyes shut to accompany his description with appropriate action, when he started violently, in common with the rest of the company, and hurried back to his chair.

The cook and housemaid screamed.

'It was a knock,' said Mr. Giles, assuming perfect serenity. 'Open the door, somebody.'

Nobody moved. At last, several precautions having been taken, Mr. Giles held on fast by the tinker's arm (to prevent his running away, as he pleasantly said) and gave the word of command to open the door. Brittles obeyed; the group, peeping timorously over each other's shoulders, beheld no more formidable object than poor little Oliver Twist, speechless and exhausted, who raised his heavy eyes and mutely solicited their compassion.

'A boy!' exclaimed Mr. Giles, valiantly pushing the tinker into the background. 'What's the matter with the—eh?— Why Brittles, look here—don't you know?'

Brittles, who had got behind the door to open it, no sooner saw Oliver than he uttered a loud cry. Mr. Giles, seizing the boy by one leg and one arm (fortunately not the broken limb) lugged him straight into the hall and deposited him at full length on the floor thereof.

'Here he is!' bawled Giles. 'Here's one of the thieves, miss! Here's a thief, wounded! I shot him, miss.'

The two women-servants ran upstairs to carry the intelligence that Mr. Giles had captured a robber, and the tinker busied himself in endeavouring to restore Oliver, lest he should die before he could be hanged. In the midst of all this noise and commotion, there was heard a sweet female voice, which quelled it in an instant.

'Giles!' whispered the voice from the stair-head.

'I'm here, miss,' replied Mr. Giles. 'Don't be frightened, miss, I ain't much injured. He didn't make a very desperate resistance, miss! I was soon too many for him.'

'Hush!' replied the young lady, 'you frighten my aunt as much as the thieves did. Is the poor creature much hurt?'

'Wounded desperate, miss,' replied Giles, with indescribable complacency.

With a footstep as soft and gentle as the voice, the speaker tripped away. She soon returned, with the direction that the wounded person was to be carried carefully up to Mr. Giles's room, and that Brittles was to saddle the pony and betake himself instantly to Chertsey, from which place he was to despatch, with all speed, a constable and a doctor.

In a handsome room (though its furniture had rather the air of old-fashioned comfort rather than of modern elegance) there sat two ladies at a well-spread breakfast table. Mr. Giles, dressed with scrupulous care in a full suit of black, was in attendance upon them.

Of the two ladies, one was well advanced in years; but the high-backed oaken chair in which she sat was not more upright than she. Dressed with the utmost nicety and precision of by-gone costume, she sat, in a stately manner, with her hands folded on the table before her. Her eyes (and age had dimmed but little of their brightness) were attentively fixed upon her young companion.

She was not past seventeen, cast in so slight and exquisite a mould, so mild and gentle, so pure and beautiful that earth seemed not her element, nor its rough creatures her fit companions. Chancing to raise her eyes as the elder lady was rearding her, she playfully put back her hair, which was simply braided on her forehead, and threw into her beaming look such an expression of affection and artless loveliness that blessed spirits might have smiled to look upon her.

'And Brittles has been gone upwards of an hour, has he?' asked the old lady, after a pause.

'An hour and twelve minutes, ma'am,' replied Mr. Giles referring to a silver watch, which he drew forth by a black ribbon.

'He is always slow,' remarked the old lady.

Mr. Giles was apparently considering the propriety of indulging in a respectful smile, when a gig drove up to the garden gate, out of which there jumped a fat gentleman who ran straight up to the door, and who, getting quickly into the house by some mysterious process, burst into the room and nearly overturned Mr. Giles and the breakfast table together.

'I never heard of such a thing!' exclaimed the fat gentleman. 'My dear Mrs. Maylie—bless my soul—in the silence of night, too—I never heard of such a thing!'

With these expressions of condolence, the fat gentleman shook hands with both ladies and, drawing up a chair, enquired how they found themselves.

The doctor seemed especially troubled by the fact of the robbery having been unexpected, and attempted in the night-time; as if it were the established custom of gentlemen in the housebreaking way to transact business at noon, and to make an appointment, by post, a day or two previous.

'And you, Miss Rose,' said the doctor turning to the young lady, 'I——'

'Oh, very much so indeed,' said Rose, interrupting him, 'but there is a poor creature upstairs whom aunt wishes you to see.'

'Ah, to be sure,' replied the doctor, 'so there is. That was your handiwork, Giles, I understand.'

Mr. Giles, who had been feverishly putting the tea-cups to rights, blushed very red and said that he had had that honour.

'Where is he?' asked the doctor. 'Show me the way. I'll look in again as I come down, Mrs. Maylie. That's the little window that he got in at, eh? Well, I couldn't have believed it!'

Talking all the way, he followed Mr. Giles upstairs; and while he is going upstairs the reader may be informed that Mr. Losberne, a surgeon in the neighbourhood, known through a circuit of ten miles round as 'the doctor', had grown fat more from good humour than from good living, and was as kind and hearty and withal as eccentric an old bachelor as will be found in five times that space by any explorer alive.

The doctor was absent much longer than either he or the ladies anticipated. At length he returned and in reply to an anxious inquiry after his patient, looked very mysterious and closed the door carefully.

'This is a very extraordinary thing, Mrs. Maylie,' said the doctor, standing with his back to the door, as if to keep it shut.

'He is not in danger, I hope?' said the old lady.

'Why, that would *not* be an extraordinary thing under the circumstances,' replied the doctor, 'though I don't think he is. Have you seen this thief?'

'No,' rejoined the old lady.

'Nor heard anything about him?'

'No.'

'Then I think it is necessary,' said the doctor; 'at all events I am quite sure you would deeply regret not having done so if you postponed it. He is perfectly quiet and comfortable now. Allow me—Miss Rose, will you permit me? Not the slightest fear, I pledge you my honour.'

With many loquacious assurances that they would be agreeably surprised in the aspect of the criminal, the doctor led them, with much ceremony and stateliness upstairs.

'Now,' said the doctor in a whisper, as he softly turned the handle of a bedroom door, 'let us hear what you think of him. He has not been shaved very recently.'

Stepping before them he gently drew back the curtains of the bed. Upon it, lieu of the dogged, black-visaged ruffian they had expected to behold, there lay a mere child, worn with pain and exhaustion and sunk into a deep sleep. The younger lady glided softly past and, seating herself in a chair by the bedside, gathered Oliver's hair from his face. As she stooped over him, her tears fell upon his face.

The boy stirred and smiled in his sleep.

'What can this mean?' exclaimed the elder lady. 'This poor child can never have been the pupil of robbers!'

'Can you—oh! can you really believe that this delicate boy has been the voluntary associate of the worst outcasts of society?' said Rose.

The surgeon shook his head, in a manner which intimated that he feared it was very possible; and observing that they might disturb the patient, led the way into an adjoining apartment.

'But even if he has been wicked,' pursued Rose, 'think how young he is; have pity upon him before it is too late!'

'My dear love,' said the elder lady, as she folded the weeping girl to her bosom, 'do you think I would harm a hair of his head?'

'Oh, no!' replied Rose eagerly.

'No, surely,' said the old lady, 'my days are drawing to their close; and may mercy be shown to me as I show it to others. What can I do to save him, sir?'

'Let me think, ma'am,' said the doctor; 'let me think.'

Mr. Losberne thrust his hands into his pockets and took several turns up and down the room, often stopping and balancing himself on his toes and frowning frightfully. After various exclamations of 'I've got it now' and 'no, I haven't', and as many renewals of the walking and frowning, he at length made a dead halt and spoke as follows:

'I think if you give me a full and unlimited commission to bully Giles and that little boy, Brittle, I can manage it. You don't object to that?'

'Unless there is some other way of preserving the child,' replied Mrs. Maylie.

'There is no other,' said the doctor; 'no other, take my word for it. This boy will wake in an hour or so, I dare say, and although I have told that thick-headed constable fellow downstairs that he mustn't be moved or spoken to, on peril of his life, I think we may converse with him without danger. Now I make this stipulation—that I shall examine him in your presence, and that, if from what he says, we judge, and I can show to the satisfaction of your cool reason, that he is a real and thorough bad one (which is more than possible) he shall be left to his fate, without any further interference on my part, at all events.'

After protests from Rose the treaty was entered into; and the parties thereunto sat down to wait, with some impatience till Oliver should awake.

It was evening before the kind-hearted doctor brought them the intelligence that he was at length sufficiently restored to be spoken to. The boy was very ill, he said, and weak from the loss of blood; but his mind was so troubled with anxiety to disclose something that he deemed it better to give him the opportunity.

The conference was a long one. Oliver told them all his simple history, and was often compelled to stop by pain and want of strength. His pillow was smoothed by gentle hands that night; and loveliness and virtue watched him as he slept. He felt calm and happy and could have died without a murmur.

The momentous interview was no sooner concluded and Oliver composed to rest again, than the doctor, after wiping his eyes and condemning them for being weak all at once, betook himself downstairs to open upon Mr. Giles. And finding nobody about the parlours, it occurred to him that perhaps he could originate the proceedings with better effect in the kitchen; so into the kitchen he went. There, all the staff—and the tinker and constable—were gathered.

'Sit still,' said the doctor, waving his hand.

'Thank you, sir,' said Mr. Giles. 'How is the patient to-night, sir?'

'So-so,' returned the doctor. 'I am afraid you have got yourself into a scrape there, Mr. Giles. Are you a Protestant?'

'Yes, sir, I hope so,' faltered Mr. Giles, who had turned very pale.

'And what are you, boy?' said the doctor sharply, turning upon Brittles.

'Lord bless me, sir!' replied Brittles, starting violently; 'I'm—the same as Mr. Giles, sir.'

'Then tell me this,' said the doctor, 'both of you, both of you! Are you going to take upon yourselves to swear that that boy upstairs is the boy that was put through the little window last night? Out with it! Come! It's a simple question of identity, you will observe.'

'That's what it is, sir,' replied the constable, nodding

profoundly. He said, if that wasn't the law, he would be glad to know what was.

'I ask you again,' thundered the doctor, 'are you, on your solemn oaths, able to identify that boy?'

Brittles looked doubtfully at Mr. Giles; Mr. Giles looked doubtfully at Brittles; the constable put his hand behind his ear to catch the reply; the two women and the tinker leaned forward to listen; the doctor glanced keenly round—when a ring was heard at the gate, and at the same moment the sound of wheels.

'It's the runners!' cried Brittles, taking up a candle. 'Me and Mr. Giles sent for them this morning.'

'What?' cried the doctor.

'Yes,' replied Brittles; 'I sent a message up by the coachman, and I only wonder they weren't here before, sir.'

'You did, did you? Then confound your—slow coaches down here; that's all,' said the doctor, walking away.

'Who's that?' inquired Brittles, opening the door a little way, with the chain up, and peeping out, shading the candle with his hand.

'Open the door,' replied a man outside; 'it's the officers from Bow Street, as was sent for today.'

The man who had knocked at the door was a stout personage of middle height, aged about fifty, with shiny black hair, cropped pretty close, half-whiskers, a round face, and sharp eyes. The other was a red-headed, bony man, in topboots, with a rather ill-favoured countenance and a turned-up rather sinister-looking nose.

'Tell your governor that Blathers and Duff is here, will you?' said the stouter man, smoothing down his hair and laying a pair of handcuffs on the table. 'Oh! Good evening, master. Can I have a word or two with you in private, please?'

This was addressed to Mr. Losberne, who now made his appearance; that gentleman, motioning Brittles to retire, brought in the two ladies and shut the door.

'This is the lady of the house,' said Mr. Losberne, motioning towards Mrs. Maylie.

Mr. Blathers made a bow.

'Now, with regard to this here robbery, master,' he said, 'what are the circumstances?'

Mr. Losberne, who appeared to be desirous of gaining time, recounted them at great length and with much circumlocution. Messrs. Blathers and Duff looked very knowing meanwhile and occasionally exchanged a nod.

'I can't say for certain, till I see the work, of course,' said Blathers, 'but my opinion at once is—I don't mind committing myself to that extent—that this wasn't done by a yokel, eh, Duff?'

'Certainly not,' replied Duff.

'Now, what is this, about this here boy that the servants are a-talking on?' said Blathers.

'Nothing at all,' replied the doctor. 'One of the frightened servants chose to take it into his head that he had something to do with this attempt to break into the house; but it's nonsense, sheer absurdity.'

'Wery easy disposed of, if it is,' remarked Duff.

'What he says is quite correct.' observed Blathers, nodding his head in a confirmatory way and playing carelessly with the handcuffs, as if they were a pair of castanets. 'Who is the boy? What account does he give of himself? Where did he come from? He didn't drop out of the clouds, did he, master?'

'Of course not,' replied the doctor, with a nervous glance at the two ladies. 'I know his whole history, but we can talk about that presently. You would like first to see the place where the thieves made their attempt, I suppose?'

'Certainly,' rejoined Mr. Blathers. 'We had better inspect the premises first. That's the usual way of doing business.'

Meanwhile the doctor walked up and down the next room in a very uneasy state; and Mrs. Maylie and Rose looked on with anxious faces.

'Upon my word,' he said, making a halt, after a great number of very rapid turns. 'I hardly know what to do.'

'Surely,' said Rose, 'the poor child's story, faithfully repeated to these men, will be sufficient to exonerate him.'

'I believe it, strange as it is, and perhaps I may be an old fool for doing so,' rejoined the doctor; 'but I don't think it is exactly the tale for a practised police officer, nevertheless.'

'Oh! What is to be done?' cried Rose. 'Dear, dear, why did they send for these people?'

'Why indeed!' exclaimed Mrs. Maylie. 'I would not have had them here for all the world.'

'All I know is,' said Mr. Losberne at last, sitting down with a kind of desperate calmness, 'that we must try and carry it off with a bold face. The boy has strong symptoms of fever upon him and is in no condition to be talked to any more; that's one comfort. Come in!'

'Well, master,' said Blathers, entering the room followed by his colleague, and making the door fast before he said any more. 'This warn't a put-up thing. We find it was a town hand, for the style of work is first-rate.'

'Wery pretty indeed, it is,' remarked Duff in an undertone.

'There was two of 'em in it,' continued Blathers, 'and they had a boy with 'em; that's plain from the size of the window. That's all to be said at present. We'll see this lad that you've got upstairs at once, if you please.'

'Perhaps they'll take something to drink first, Mrs. Maylie?' said the doctor, his face brightening as if some new thought had occurred to him.

'Oh, to be sure!' said Rose eagerly. 'You shall have it immediately, if you will.'

'Why, thank you, miss!' said Blathers, drawing his coat-sleeve across his mouth; 'it's dry work, this sort of duty. A little drop of spirits, master, if it's all the same.'

When Mr. Blathers had put down his wine-glass, Mr. Losberne, closely followed by the two officers, ascended to Oliver's bedroom, Mr. Giles preceding the party with a lighted candle.

Oliver had been dozing, but looked worse and was more feverish than he had appeared yet. Being assisted by the doctor, he managed to sit up in bed for a minute or so; and looked at the strangers without at all understanding what was going forward—in fact, without seeming to recollect where he was or what had been passing.

'This,' said Mr. Losberne, speaking softly, but with great vehemence notwithstanding, 'this is the lad, who being accidentally wounded by a spring gun in some boyish trespass on Mr. What-d'ye-call-him's grounds at the back here, comes to the house for assistance this morning, and is immediately laid hold of and maltreated by that ingenious gentleman with the candle in his hand, who has placed his life in considerable danger, as I can professionally certify.'

Messrs. Blather and Duff looked at Mr. Giles, as he was thus recommended to their notice. The bewildered butler gazed from them towards Oliver, and from Oliver towards Mr. Losberne, with a most ludicrous mixture of fear and perplexity. He then stammered that Oliver was not the boy with the burglars.

'Has this man been a-drinking, sir?' inquired Blathers turning to the doctor.

'What a precious muddle-headed chap you are!' said Duff, addressing Mr. Giles with supreme contempt.

Mr. Losberne had been feeling the patient's pulse during this short dialogue; but he now rose from the chair by the bedside and remarked that if the officers had any doubts on the subject, they would perhaps like to step into the next room and have Brittles before them.

Acting upon this suggestion, they adjourned to a neighbouring apartment, where Mr. Brittles being called in, involved himself and his respected superior in such a wonderful maze of fresh contradictions and impossibilities, that finally, the officers, without troubling themselves very much about Oliver, left the Chertsey constable in the house and took up their rest for that night in the town, promising to return next morning.

After some more examination and great deal more conversation, a neighbouring magistrate was readily induced to take the joint bail of Mrs. Maylie and Mr. Losberne for Oliver's appearance if he should ever be called upon; and Blathers and Duff, being rewarded with a couple of guineas, returned to town with divided opinions on the subject of their expedition.

Oliver's ailings were neither slight nor few. In addition to the pain and delay attendant on a broken limb, his exposure to the wet and cold had brought on fever and ague, which hung about him for many weeks and reduced him sadly. But at length he began, by slow degrees, to get better and to be able to say sometimes, in a few tearful words, how deeply he felt the goodness of the two sweet ladies, and how ardently he hoped that when he grew strong and well again he could do something to show his gratitude.

'Poor fellow!' said Rose, when Oliver had been one day feebly endeavouring to utter the words of thankfulness that rose to his pale lips; 'you shall have many opportunities of serving us if you will. We are going into the country, and my aunt intends that you should accompany us. The quiet place, the pure air, and all the pleasures and beauties of Spring, will restore you in a few days. We will employ you in a hundred ways when you can bear the trouble.'

'The trouble!' cried Oliver. 'Oh, dear lady, if I could but work for you! If I could only give you pleasure by watering your flowers, or watching your birds, or running up and down the whole day long to make you happy! What would I give to do it?'

'You shall give nothing at all,' said Miss Maylie, smiling.

'But I was thinking that I am ungrateful now,' said Oliver.

'To whom?' inquired the young lady.

'To the kind gentleman and the dear old nurse, who took so much care of me before,' rejoined Oliver. 'If they knew how happy I am, they would be pleased, I am sure.'

'I am sure they would,' rejoined Oliver's benefactress, 'and Mr. Losberne has already been kind enough to promise that when you are well enough to bear the journey, he will carry you to see them.'

'Has he, ma'am?' cried Oliver, his face brightening with pleasure. 'I don't know what I shall do for joy when I see their kind faces again!'

In a short time Oliver was sufficiently recovered to undergo the fatigue of this expedition. One morning he and Mr. Losberne set out, accordingly, in a little carriage which belonged to Mrs. Maylie. When they came to Chertsey Bridge, Oliver turned very pale and uttered a loud exclamation.

'That, sir,' cried Oliver, pointing out of the carriage window, 'that house.'

'Yes; well, what of it? Stop, coachman, pull up here,' cried the doctor. 'What of the house, my man, eh?'

'The thieves—the house they took me to!' whispered Oliver.

'The devil it is!' cried the doctor. 'Holloa, there! Let me out'!

But, before the coachman could dismount from his box, he

had tumbled out of the coach, by some means or other, and running down to the deserted tenement, began kicking at the door like a madman.

'Halloa?' said a little ugly hump-backed man, opening the door. 'What's the matter here?'

'Where's Sikes?' exclaimed the doctor, without a moment's reflection. 'Where's Sikes, you thief?'

'You take yourself off before I do you a mischief,' growled the hunchback. 'I've lived here five-and-twenty years and all alone.'

'The boy must have made a mistake,' muttered the doctor to himself, and flinging the hunchback a piece of money, he returned to the carriage.

The man followed to the chariot door, and as Mr. Losberne turned to speak to the driver, he looked into the carriage and eyed Oliver for an instant with a glance so sharp and vindictive that, waking or sleeping, he could not forget it for months afterwards.

As Oliver knew the name of the street in which Mr. Brownlow resided, they were now enabled to drive straight thither.

'Now, my boy, which house is it?' inquired Mr. Losberne.

'That! That!' replied Oliver, eagerly pointing out of the window. 'The white house. Oh, make haste! Pray make haste!'

The coach rolled on. It stopped. No, that was the wrong house; the next door. It went on a few paces and stopped again. Oliver looked up at the windows with tears of happy expectation coursing down his face.

Alas! The white house was empty and there was a bill in the window: 'To Let'.

'Knock at the next door,' cried Mr. Losberne, taking Oliver's arm in his. 'What has become of Mr. Brownlow, who used to live in the adjoining house, do you know?'

The servant said that Mr. Brownlow had sold off his goods and gone to the West Indies, six weeks before. Oliver clasped his hands and sank feebly backward.

'Has his housekeeper gone too?' inquired Mr. Losberne, after a moment's pause.

'Yes, sir,' replied the servant. 'The old gentleman, the

housekeeper, and a gentleman who was a friend of Mr. Brownlow's all went together.'

This bitter disappointment caused Oliver much sorrow and grief even in the midst of his happiness.

The circumstance occasioned no alteration, however, in the behaviour of his benefactors. After another fortnight, they made preparations for quitting the house at Chertsey for some months. Sending the plate, which had so excited Fagin's cupidity, to the banker's, and leaving Giles and another servant in care of the house, they departed to a cottage at some distance in the country, and took Oliver with them.

Who can describe the pleasure and delight, the peace of mind and soft tranquillity, the sickly boy felt in the balmy air and among the green hills and rich woods of an inland village?

So three months glided away; three months, which in the life of the most blessed and favoured of mortals, might have been unmingled happiness, and which, in Oliver's were true felicity. With the purest and most amiable generosity on one side, and the truest, warmest, soul-felt gratitude on the other, it is no wonder that by the end of that short time Oliver Twist had become completely domesticated with the old lady and her niece, and that the fervent attachment of his young and sensitive heart was repaid by their pride in and attachment to himself.

The same quiet life went on at the little cottage, and the same cheerful serenity prevailed among its inmates until one beautiful night when they had taken a longer walk than was customary for them. Rose had been in high spirits, but on returning home fell into a low and very solemn air, then gave a shudder as though some deadly chillness were passing over her.

'I fear I am ill, aunt,' she said weakly, and she was indeed, for when morning came she was in the first stage of a high and dangerous fever.

'This letter must be sent with all possible expedition to Mr. Losberne,' said Mrs. Maylie to Oliver. 'It must be carried to the market town four miles off and thence despatched, by an express or horseback, straight to Chertsey by the people at the inn.'

Oliver started off without more delay, at the greatest speed he could muster, nor did he stop until he came, in a great heat and covered with dust, to the sign of 'The George' in the market-place. Here in a desperate state of impatience and anxiety Oliver watched the landlord arrange for the speedy delivery of his letter by a man who set spurs to his horse and was out of the town in a couple of minutes.

Oliver hurried up the innyard with a somewhat lighter heart and was turning out of the gateway when he accidentally stumbled against a tall man wrapped in a cloak.

'What the devil's this?' cried the man, glaring at the boy with his large dark eyes. 'Who would have thought it? Grind him to ashes! He'd start up from a stone coffin to come in my way!'

'I am sorry,' stammered Oliver, confused by the strange man's wild look. 'I hope I have not hurt you!'

'Rot you!' murmured the man in a horrible passion. 'If I had only had the courage to say the word, I might have been free of you in a night. Curse on your head, you imp!'

The man shook his fist and advanced towards Oliver who turned his face homewards, running as fast as he could, but the circumstance did not dwell in his recollection long for when he reached the cottage there was enough to occupy his mind.

Rose Maylie had rapidly grown worse; before midnight she was delirious. Morning came, and the little cottage was lonely and still. Late at night, Mr. Losberne arrived. 'It is hard,' said the good doctor; 'so young, so much beloved, but there is very little hope.'

Another morning—the fair young creature lay, wasting fast. Oliver crept away to the old churchyard and, sitting down on one of the green mounds, wept and prayed for her in silence.

When he reached home, he learnt that she had fallen into a deep sleep from which she would waken either to recovery and life, or to bid them farewell and die. With Mrs. Maylie he sat listening, afraid to speak, for hours, until their quick ears caught the sound of an approaching footstep and Mr. Losberne entered.

'As God is good and merciful,' cried the doctor passionately, 'she will live to bless us all for years to come.'

The old lady fell upon her knees in thankfulness; Oliver could not weep or speak or rest until, after a long ramble in the quiet evening air, he seemed to awaken to a full sense of the joyful change that had occurred.

The night was fast closing in when he returned homeward, laden with flowers which he had culled, with peculiar care, for the adornment of the sick chamber. As he walked briskly along the road he heard behind him the noise of some vehicle approaching at a furious pace. Looking round, he saw it was a post-chaise, driven at great speed; and as the horses were galloping, and the road was narrow, he stood leaning against a gate until it should have passed him.

As it dashed on, Oliver caught a glimpse of a man in a white nightcap, and a stentorian voice bellowed to the driver to stop, which he did as soon as he could pull up his horses. Then the nightcap once again appeared and the same voice called Oliver by his name.

'Here!' cried the voice, 'Oliver, what's the news? Miss Rose, Master O-li-ver!'

'Is it you, Giles?' cried Oliver, running up to the chaise door.

Giles popped out his nightcap again, preparatory to making some reply, when he was suddenly pulled back by a young gentleman who occupied the other corner of the chaise and who eagerly demanded what was the news.

'In a word,' cried the gentleman, 'better or worse?'

'Better—much better!' replied Oliver hastily.

'Thank heaven!' exclaimed the gentleman. 'You are sure?'

'Quite, sir,' replied Oliver. 'The change took place only a few hours ago, and Mr. Losberne says that all danger is at an end.'

The gentleman said not another word, but opening the chaise door, leaped out.

'I think you had better go on to my mother's in the chaise, Giles. I would rather walk slowly on so as to gain a little time before I see her. You can say I am coming.'

'I beg your pardon, Mr. Harry,' said Giles, who had been wiping his eyes with a blue cotton handkerchief dotted with white spots, 'but if you would leave the postboy to say that, I should be very much obliged to you. It wouldn't be proper for the maids to see me in this state, sir; I should never have any more authority with them if they did.

Mr. Giles, reminded of his unbecoming costume, snatched off and pocketed his nightcap and substituted a hat of grave and sober shape, which he took out of the chaise. This done, the postboy drove off; Giles, Mr. Maylie and Oliver followed at their leisure.

As they walked along, Oliver glanced from time to time with much interest at the newcomer. He seemed about five and twenty years of age, and was of the middle height; his countenance was frank and handsome, and his demeanour easy and prepossessing. Notwithstanding the difference between youth and age, he bore so strong a likeness to the old lady that Oliver would have had no great difficulty in imagining their relationship if he had not already spoken of her as his mother.

Mrs. Maylie was anxiously waiting to receive her son when he reached the cottage. The meeting did not take place without great emotion on both sides.

'Mother!' whispered the young man, 'why did you not write before?'

'I did,' replied Mrs. Maylie, 'but on reflection, I determined to keep back the letter until I had heard Mr. Losberne's opinion.'

'But why?' said the young man. 'If Rose had—I cannot utter that word now—how could you ever have forgiven yourself? How could I ever have known happiness again? The mental agony I have suffered during the last two days wrings from me the avowal to you of a passion which, as you well know, is not one of yesterday, nor one I have lightly formed. On Rose, sweet gentle girl, my heart is set as firmly as ever heart of man was set on woman. Mother, if you oppose me in this great stake, you take my peace and happiness in your hands and cast them to the winds.'

'Harry,' said Mrs. Maylie, 'before you stake your all on this chance, reflect for a few moments, my dear child, on Rose's history, and consider what effect the knowledge of her doubtful birth may have on her decision, devoted as she is to us, with all the intensity of her noble mind, and with that perfect sacrifice of self which has always been her characteristic.'

'What do you mean?'

'That I leave you to discover,' replied Mrs. Maylie. 'Now I must go back to her and I will tell her all you feel.'

Mr. Losberne and Oliver had remained at another end of the apartment while this hurried conversation was proceeding. The former now held out his hand to Harry Maylie, and hearty salutations were exchanged between them. The doctor then communicated in reply to multifarious questions from his young friend, a precise account of his patient's situation, which was quite as consolatory and full of promise as Oliver's statement had encouraged him to hope, and to the whole of which Mr. Giles, who affected to be busy about the luggage, listened with greedy ears. The kitchen was later speedily enlightened likewise.

Oliver rose next morning in better heart, and went about his usual early occupations with more hope and pleasure than he had known for many days. Time did not hang heavily on his hands, for he applied himself with redoubled assiduity to the books from which he now received instructions at the hands of a white-headed old gentleman. It was while he was engaged in this pursuit that he was greatly startled and distressed by a most unexpected occurrence.

One beautiful evening when the first shades of twilight were beginning to settle upon the earth, Oliver sat, intent on his books, at the window of his little room on the ground-floor at the back of the house. He had been poring over them for some time; and as the day had been uncommonly sultry, and he had exerted himself a great deal, it is no disparagement to the authors, whoever they may have been, to say that gradually and by slow degrees he fell asleep.

There is a kind of sleep that steals upon us sometimes, which, while it holds the body prisoner, does not free the mind from a sense of things about it. Oliver knew perfectly well that he was in his own little room, that his books were lying on the table before him, that the sweet air was stirring among the creeping plants outside. And yet he was asleep. Suddenly the scene changed; the air became close and confined; and he thought with a glow of terror that he was in the Jew's house again. There sat the hideous old man in his accustomed corner, pointing at him and whispering to another man, with his face averted, who sat beside him.

'Hush, my dear,' he thought he heard the Jew say; 'it is he sure enough. Come away.'

'He!' the other man seemed to answer; 'could I mistake him, think you?'

The man seemed to say this with such dreadful hatred that Oliver awoke with the fear and started up.

Good Heaven! What was that which sent the blood tingling to his heart, and deprived him of his voice and power to move! There—there—at the window—close before him—so close that he could have almost touched him before he started back, with his eyes peering into the room and meeting his, there stood the Jew! And beside him, white with rage, or fear, or both, were the scowling features of the very man who had accosted him in the innyard.

It was but an instant, a glance, a flash, before his eyes, and they were gone. But they had recognized him and he them; and their look was as firmly impressed upon his memory as if it had been deeply carved in stone and set before him from birth. He stood transfixed for a moment; then leaping from the window into the garden, called loudly for help.

The inmates of the house found him pale and agitated, pointing in the direction of the meadows behind the house, and scarcely able to articulate the words, 'The Jew! The Jew!'

Mr. Giles was at a loss to comprehend what this outcry meant; but Harry Maylie, whose perceptions were something quicker, and who had heard Oliver's history from his mother, understood it at once.

'What direction did he take?' he asked, catching up a heavy stick which was standing in a corner.

'That,' replied Oliver, pointing out the course the man had taken, 'I missed them in an instant.'

Harry sprang over the hedge and darted off; Giles and Oliver followed, and Mr. Losberne, who had been out walking, tumbled over the hedge after them, but the search was all in vain though only with the coming on of night did they give up with reluctance. After a few days the affair began to be forgotten, as most affairs are when wonder, having no fresh food to support it, dies away of itself.

Meantime Rose was rapidly recovering. She had left her

room, was able to go out and, mixing once more with the family, carried joy into the hearts of all.

But although this happy change had a visible effect on the little circle, it became evident that something was in progress which affected the peace of the young lady and of somebody else besides. At length, one morning when Rose was alone in the breakfast parlour, Harry Maylie begged permission to speak with her.

'Rose, the most cherished hopes of my heart are not unknown to you, though from my lips you have not yet heard them stated. Rose, my own dear Rose, for years I have loved you, hoping to win my way to fame and then come proudly home and tell you it had been pursued only for you to share. That time has not yet arrived; but here, with no fame won, I offer you the heart so long your own.'

There were tears in the eyes of the gentle girl as these words were spoken, but she mastered her emotion and replied firmly:

'No, Harry. I am a friendless portionless girl with a blight upon my name. The prospect before you is a brilliant one. All the honours to which great talents and powerful connections can help men in public life are in store for you. I will neither mingle with such as may hold in scorn the mother who gave me life, nor bring disgrace or failure on the son of her who has so well supplied that mother's place. There is a stain upon my name which the world visits on innocent heads. I will carry it into no blood but my own; and the reproach shall rest alone on me. And now I must leave you, indeed.'

She extended her hand, but the young man caught her to his bosom and imprinting one kiss on her beautiful forehead, hurried from the room to inform Mr. Losberne, who was that morning departing for Chertsey, that he would be his travelling companion.

The good doctor bustled out to see the luggage packed and Harry beckoned Oliver into the window recess.

'Oliver,' he said in a low voice, 'I shall not be at home again, perhaps for some time. I wish you to write to me— say once a fortnight, on every alternate Monday—to the General Post Office in London, will you? I should like to know how—how my mother and Miss Maylie are, and whether she—they, I mean—seem happy and quite well. I would rather you did not mention it to them because it might make my mother anxious to write oftener and it is a trouble and worry to her. You understand me?'

Oliver, quite elated and honoured by a sense of his importance, faithfully promised to be secret and explicit in his communications, and Mr. Maylie took leave of him with many assurances of his regard and protection.

9

MR. AND MRS. BUMBLE MEET MR. MONKS

MR. BUMBLE sat in the workhouse parlour with his eyes moodily fixed on the cheerless grate, whence, as it was summer time, no brighter gleam proceeded than the reflection of certain sickly rays of the sun which were sent back from its cold and shining surface.

Mr. Bumble's laced coat and cocked hat, where were they? He still wore knee-breeches and dark cotton stockings on his nether limbs, but they were not *the* breeches. The coat was wide-skirted and in that respect like *the* coat, but, oh, how different! The mighty cocked hat was replaced by a modest round one. Mr. Bumble was no longer a beadle. In fact, he had married Mrs. Corney and was master of the workhouse. Another beadle had come into power. On him the cocked hat, gold-laced coat, and staff had all three descended.

'And tomorrow two months it was done!' said Mr. Bumble with a sigh. 'It seems a age. I sold myself for six teaspoons, a pair of sugar tongs, and a milk-pot, with a small quantity of second-hand furniture and twenty pound in money. I went very reasonable. Cheap, dirt cheap!'

'Cheap!' cried a shrill voice in Mr. Bumble's ear: 'you would have been dear at any price; and dear enough I paid for you, Lord above knows that!'

'Mrs. Bumble, ma'am!' said Mr. Bumble with sentimental sternness.

'Well!' cried the lady.

'Have the goodness to look at me,' said Mr. Bumble, fixing his eyes upon her.

The matter of fact is that the matron was in no way overpowered by Mr. Bumble's scowl, but on the contrary, treated it with great disdain, and even raised a laugh thereat which sounded as if it were genuine.

On hearing this most unexpected sound, Mr. Bumble

looked, first incredulous, and afterwards amazed. He then relapsed into his former state, nor did he arouse himself until his attention was again awakened by the voice of his partner.

'Are you going to sit snoring there all day?' inquired Mrs. Bumble.

'I shall sit here as long as I think proper, ma'am, and I shall snore, gape, sneeze, laugh, or cry, as the humour strikes me.'

Mrs. Bumble, seeing that a blow for mastership must be struck, dropped into a chair and with a loud scream that Mr. Bumble was a hard-hearted brute, fell into a paroxysm of tears.

But tears were not the things to find their way to Mr. Bumble's soul; his heart was waterproof.

'Cry away,' he said. 'It opens the lungs, washes the countenance, exercises the eyes, and softens down the temper.'

Now, Mrs. Corney that was, had tried the tears because they were less troublesome than a manual assault; but she was quite prepared to make trial of the latter mode of proceeding, as Mr. Bumble was not long in discovering.

Clasping him tightly round the throat with one hand, the expect lady inflicted a shower of blows upon his head with the other. This done, she created a little variety by scratching his face and tearing his hair, before pushing him over with a chair.

'Get up!' said Mrs. Bumble in a voice of command. 'And take yourself away from here unless you want me to do something desperate.'

Mr. Bumble rose with a very rueful countenance, wondering much what something desperate might be. Picking up his hat he looked towards the door.

'Are you going?' demanded Mrs. Bumble.

'Certainly, my dear, certainly,' rejoined Mr. Bumble, making a quicker motion towards the door.

Mr. Bumble was fairly taken by surprise and fairly beaten. He had a decided propensity for bullying, derived no inconsiderable pleasure from the exercise of petty cruelty, and consequently was (it is needless to say) a coward. He walked distractedly into the street and, after passing a great many public-houses, at length stepped into one whose parlour was deserted save by one solitary customer.

He had the air of a stranger, and seemed, by a certain haggardness in his look, as well as by the dusty soils on his dress, to have travelled some distance. He eyed Bumble askance.

'I have seen you before, I think,' said he eventually. 'You were differently dressed at that time, and I only passed you in the street, but I should know you again. You were beadle here once, were you not?'

'I was,' said Mr. Bumble in some surprise, 'porochial beadle.'

'Just so,' rejoined the other, nodding his head, 'it was in that character I saw you. What are you now?'

'Master of the workhouse,' rejoined Mr. Bumble.

'You have the same eye to your own interest that you always had, I doubt not,' resumed the stranger, looking keenly into Mr. Bumble's eyes, as he raised them in astonishment at the question. 'Don't scruple to answer freely, man, I know you pretty well, you see.'

'I suppose a married man,' replied Mr. Bumble, shading his eyes with his hand, and surveying the stranger from head to foot, in evident perplexity, 'is not more averse to turning an honest penny when he can, than a single one. Porochial officers are not so well paid that they can afford to refuse any little extra fee, when it comes to them in a civil and proper manner.'

The stranger smiled and nodded his head again, as if to say he had not mistaken his man, then rang the bell and ordered Mr. Bumble a drink.

'Now listen to me,' said the stranger, after closing the door and window. 'I came down to this place today to find you out; and, by one of those chances which the devil throws in the way of his friends sometimes, you walked into the very room I was sitting in, while you were uppermost in my mind. I want some information from you. I don't ask you to give it for nothing, slight as it is. Put up that, to begin with.'

As he spoke he pushed a couple of sovereigns across the table to his companion, carefully, as though unwilling that the clinking of money should be heard without. When Mr. Bumble had scrupulously examined the coins to see if they were genuine, and had put them up, with much satisfaction, in his waistcoat pocket, he went on:

'Carry your memory back—let me see—twelve years last winter. A boy was born in the workhouse.'

'Many boys,' observed Mr. Bumble, shaking his head despondingly.

'A murrain on the young devils!' cried the stranger. 'I speak of one—a meek-looking, pale-faced boy, who was apprenticed down here to a coffin-maker—I wish he had made his coffin and screwed his body in it—and who afterwards ran away to London, as it was supposed.'

'Why, you mean Oliver! Young Twist!' said Mr. Bumble; 'I remember him of course. There wasn't a obstinater young rascal——'

'It's not of him I want to hear; I've heard enough of him,' said the stranger. 'It's of a woman—the hag that nursed his mother. Where is she?'

'She died last winter,' rejoined Mr. Bumble.

For a while the stranger seemed lost in thought; then he rose, as if to depart.

But Mr. Bumble was cunning enough; and he at once saw that an opportunity was opened for the lucrative disposal of some secret in the possession of his better half. Hastily calling this circumstance to mind, he informed the stranger with an air of mystery that one woman had been closeted with the old harridan shortly before she died, and that she could, as he had reason to believe, throw some light on the subject of his inquiry. Only through him could he meet her.

'Right,' said the stranger, producing a scrap of paper and writing down upon it an obscure address by the water-side. 'Bring her to me there tomorrow, at nine—in the evening. I needn't tell you to be secret. It's your interest.'

'What name am I to ask for?' said Mr. Bumble.

'Monks!' rejoined the man, and strode away.

It was a dull, close, overcast summer evening. The clouds seemed to presage a violent thunderstorm, when Mr. and Mrs. Bumble, turning out of the main street of the town, directed their course towards a scattered little colony of ruinous houses, distant from it some mile and a half, or thereabouts, and erected on a low unwholesome swamp bordering upon the river. They reached a ruined building, which had been a factory, and paused as the first peal of distant thunder reverberated in the air, and the rain commenced pouring violently down.

'The place should be somewhere here,' said Bumble, consulting a scrap of paper he held in his hand.

'Holloa there!' cried a voice from above. 'I'll be with you directly,' with which the head disappeared and the door closed.

'Is that the man?' asked Mr. Bumble's good lady.

Mr. Bumble nodded in the affirmative.

'Then mind what I told you,' said the matron, 'and be careful to say as little as you can, or you'll betray us at once.'

Mr. Bumble, who had eyed the building with very rueful looks, was apparently about to express some doubts when Monks opened a small door near which they stood and beckoned them inwards.

'Come in!' he cried impatiently, stamping his foot upon the ground. 'Don't keep me here! This is the woman, is it?'

'Hem! That is the woman,' replied Mr. Bumble, mindful of his wife's caution.

Bestowing something halfway between a smile and a frown upon his two companions, and again beckoning them to follow him, the man hastened across the apartment, which was of considerable extent, but low in the roof. He led the way up a ladder and, hastily closing the window-shutter of the room into which it led, lowered a lantern which hung at the end of a rope and pulley passed through one of the heavy beams in the ceiling, and which cast a dim light up on an old table and three chairs that were placed beneath it.

'Now,' said Monks, when they had all three seated themselves, 'the sooner we come to our business the better for all. The woman knows what it is, does she?'

The question was addressed to Bumble, but his wife anticipated the reply by intimating that she was perfectly acquainted with it.

'He is right in saying that you were with this hag the night she died, and that she told you something——'

'About the mother of the boy you named,' replied the matron interrupting him, 'yes.'

'The question is, of what nature was her communication?' said Monks.

'That's the second,' observed the woman, with much deliberation. 'The first is, what may the communication be worth?'

'Who the devil can tell that, without knowing of what kind it is?' asked Monks.

'Nobody better than you, I am persuaded,' answered Mrs. Bumble, who did not want for spirit, as her yoke-fellow could abundantly testify.

'Humph!' said Monks significantly, and with a look of eager inquiry; 'there may be money's worth to get, eh?'

'What's it worth to you?' asked the woman collectedly.

'It may be nothing, it may be twenty pounds,' replied Monks. 'Speak out and let me know which.'

'Add five pounds to the sum you have named; give me five-and-twenty pounds in gold; and I'll tell you all I know. Not before.'

'Five-and-twenty pounds!' exclaimed Monks, drawing back.

'I spoke as plainly as I could,' replied Mrs. Bumble. 'It's not a large sum, either.'

'Not a large sum for a paltry secret that may be nothing when it's told!' cried Monks impatiently; 'and which has been lying dead for twelve years past, or more!'

'Such matters keep well and, like good wine, often double their value in course of time,' answered the matron, still preserving the resolute indifference she had assumed. 'As to lying dead, there are those who will lie dead for twelve thousand years to come, or twelve million, for anything you or I know, who will tell strange tales at last!'

'What if I pay it for nothing?' asked Monks, hesitating.

'You can easily take it away again,' replied the matron. 'I am but a woman, alone here and unprotected.'

He thrust his hand into a side-pocket and, producing a canvas bag, told out twenty-five sovereigns on the table and pushed them over to the woman.

'Now,' he said, 'gather them up and let's hear your story.'

'When this woman that we called old Sally died,' the matron began, 'she and I were alone. I stood alone beside the body when death came over it.'

'Good,' said Monks, regarding her attentively, 'go on.'

'She spoke of a young creature,' resumed the matron, 'who had brought a child into the world some years before, not merely in the same room, but in the same bed in which she then lay dying. The child was the one you named to him last night,' said the matron, nodding carelessly towards her husband; 'the mother this nurse had robbed. She stole from the corpse, when it had hardly turned to one, that which the dead mother had prayed her, with her last breath, to keep for the infant's sake.'

'She sold it?' cried Monks, with desperate eagerness; 'Did she sell it? Where? When? To whom? How long before?'

'As she told me, with great difficulty, that she had done this,' said the matron, 'she fell back and died. But she clutched my gown violently, with one hand, which was partly closed; and when I saw that she was dead, and so removed the hand by force, I found it clasped a scrap of dirty paper, a pawn-broker's duplicate.'

'For what?' demanded Monks.

'In good time I'll tell you.' said the woman. 'I judge that she had kept the trinket for some time in the hope of turning it to better account, and then had pawned it. The time was out in two days; I thought something might one day come of it too, and so redeemed the pledge.'

'Where is it now?' asked Monks quickly.

'There,' replied the woman. And as if glad to be relieved of it, she hastily threw upon the table a small kid bag scarcely large enough for a French watch, which Monks pouncing upon, tore open with trembling hands. It contained a little gold locket, in which were two locks of hair and a plain gold wedding ring.

'It has the word "Agnes" engraved on the inside,' said the woman. 'There is a blank left for the surname, and then follows the date, which is within a year before the child was born. I found out that.'

'And this is all?' said Monks, after a close and eager scrutiny of the contents of the little packet.

'All,' replied the woman. 'I know nothing of the story beyond what I can guess at,' she said, addressing Monks after a short silence, 'and I want to know nothing, for it's safer not. But I may ask you two questions, may I?'

'You may ask,' said Monks, with some show of surprise, but whether I answer or not, is another question.'

'. . . which makes three,' observed Mr. Bumble, essaying a stroke of facetiousness.

'Is that what you expected to get from me?' demanded the matron.

'It is,' replied Monks. 'The other question?'

'What do you propose to do with it? Can it be used against me?'

'Never,' rejoined Monks, 'nor against me either. See here! But don't move a step forward, or your life is not worth a bulrush.'

With these words he suddenly wheeled the table aside and, pulling an iron ring in the boarding, threw back a large trap-door which opened close at Mr. Bumble's feet and caused that gentleman to retire several paces backward with great precipitation.

'Look down,' said Monks, lowering the lantern into the gulf. 'Don't fear me; I could have let you down quietly enough, when you were seated over it, if that had been my game.'

They could see the water below them.

Monks drew the little packet from his breast where he had hurriedly thrust it, and tying it to a leaden weight which had formed a part of some pulley and was lying on the floor, dropped it into the stream. It fell straight and true as a die, clove the water with a scarcely audible splash, and was gone.

The three, looking into each other's faces, seemed to breathe more freely.

'There!' said Monks, closing the trap-door, which fell heavily back into its former position. 'If the sea ever gives up its dead, as books say it will, it will keep its gold and silver to itself, and that trash among it. We have nothing more to say, and may break up our pleasant party.'

'By all means,' said Mr. Bumble, with great alacrity.

'You'll keep a quiet tongue in your head, will you?' Monks said with a threatening look.

'You may depend upon me, young man,' answered Mr.

umble, bowing himself gradually towards the ladder, with
xcessive politeness. 'On everybody's account, young man;
n my own, you know, Mr. Monks.'

'I am glad for your sake to hear it,' remarked Monks.
Light your lantern and get away from here as fast as you can.'

They were no sooner gone than Monks, who appeared to
ntertain an invincible repugnance to being left alone, called
o a boy who had been hidden somewhere below. Bidding
im go first and bear the light, he returned to the chamber he
ad just quitted.

10

NANCY WARNS ROSE MAYLIE

On the evening following that upon which the three worthic mentioned in the last chapter disposed of their little matter o business as therein narrated. Mr. William Sikes, awakening fron a nap, drowsily growled forth an inquiry what time of night it was

The room in which Mr. Sikes was situated was at no grea distance from his former lodgings. It was not in appearanc so desirable a habitation as his old quarters, being a mea and badly furnished apartment, of very limited size, lighte by only one small window in the shelving roof, and abuttin on a close and dirty lane. Nor were there wanting othe indications of a good gentleman's having gone down in th world of late.

The housebreaker was lying on his bed, wrapped in hi white greatcoat, by way of dressing gown, and displaying set of features in no degree improved by the cadaverous hu of illness, and the addition of a soiled nightcap and a stif black beard of a week's growth. The dog sat at the bedsid now eyeing his master with a wistful look, and now prickin his ears and uttering a low growl as some noise in the stree or in the lower part of the house, attracted his attentior Seated by the window, busily engaged in patching an ol waistcoat which formed a portion of the robber's ordinar dress, was a female, so pale and reduced with watching an privation that there would have been considerable difficult in recognizing her as the same Nancy who has already figure in this tale, but for the voice in which she replied to M Sikes's question.

'Not long gone seven,' said the girl. 'How do you fe tonight, Bill?'

'As weak as water,' replied Mr. Sikes, with an imprecatio on his eyes and limbs. 'Here: lend me a hand, and let me g off this thundering bed anyhow.'

Illness had not improved Mr. Sikes's temper; as the girl raised him up and led him to a chair he muttered various curses on her awkwardness and struck her. Thereupon the girl, being really weak and exhausted, dropped her head over the back of the chair and fainted. Mr. Sikes tried a little blasphemy and, finding that mode of treatment ineffectual, called for assistance.

'What's the matter here, my dear?' said Fagin, looking in.

'Lend a hand to the girl, can't you?' replied Sikes impatiently. 'Don't stand chattering and grinning at me!

With an exclamation of surprise, Fagin hastened to the girl's assistance, while Mr. John Dawkins (otherwise the Artful Dodger) who had followed his venerable friend into the room, hastily deposited on the floor a bundle with which he was laden, and snatching a bottle from the grasp of Master Charles Bates who came close at his heels, uncorked it in a twinkling with his teeth, and poured a portion of the contents down the patient's throat, previously taking a taste himself to prevent mistakes.

'Give her a whiff of fresh air with the bellows, Charlie,' said Mr. Dawkins, 'and you slap her hands, Fagin, while Bill undoes the petticuts.'

These united restoratives, administered with great energy—especially that department consigned to Master Bates, who appeared to consider his share in the proceedings a piece of unexampled pleasantry—were not long in producing the desired effect. The girl gradually recovered her senses and, staggering to a chair by the bedside, hid her face upon the pillow, leaving Mr. Sikes to confront the newcomers, in some astonishment at their unlooked for appearance.

'Why, what evil wind has blowed you here?' he asked Fagin.

'No evil wind at all, my dear, for evil winds blow nobody any good; and I've brought something good with me that you'll be glad to see. Dodger, my dear, open the bundle, and give Bill all the little trifles that we spent all our money on this morning.'

In compliance with Mr. Fagin's request, the Artful untied his bundle, which was of large size and formed of an old tablecloth, and handed the articles of food and drink it contained one by one to Charley Bates, who placed them on the table, with various econiums on their rarity and excellence.

'The things is well enough in their way,' observed Mr. Sikes, a little soothed as he glanced over the table; 'but what have you got to say for yourself? Why you should leave me here, down in the mouth, health, blunt, and everything else, and take no more notice of me all this mortal time, than if I was that 'ere dog.'

'I was away a week and more, my dear,' replied the old Jew, 'on a plant.'

'And what about the other fortnight?' demanded Sikes. 'What about the other fortnight that you've left me lying here, like a sick rat in his hole?'

'I couldn't help it, Bill; I can't go into a long explanation before company; but I couldn't help it, upon my honour.'

'Upon your what?' growled Sikes, with excessive disgust. 'Here! Cut me off a piece of that pie, one of you boys, to take the taste of that out of my mouth, or it'll choke me dead!'

Fagin, feigning an unusual show of spirits, gradually brought Mr. Sikes into a better temper by affecting to regard his threats as a little pleasant banter, and, moreover, by laughing very heartily at one or two rough jokes, which, after repeated applications to the spirit bottle, he condescended to make.

'It's all very well,' said Mr. Sikes, 'but I must have some blunt from you tonight.'

'I haven't a piece of coin about me,' replied the Jew.

'Then you've got lots at home,' retorted Sikes, 'and I must have some from there. Nancy shall go to the ken and fetch it, and I'll lie down and have a snooze while she's gone.'

After a great deal of haggling and squabbling, Fagin beat down the amount of the required advance from five pounds to three pounds four and sixpence, protesting with many solemn asseverations that that would only leave him eighteen-pence to keep house with. The Jew then, taking leave of his affectionate friend, returned homeward, attended by Nancy and the boys, Mr. Sikes, meanwhile, flinging himself on the bed and composing himself to while away the time until the young lady's return.

In due course they arrived at Fagin's abode, where they found Toby Crackit and Mr. Chitling intent upon their fifteenth game of cribbage, which it is scarcely necessary to say the latter gentleman lost, and with it his fifteenth and last sixpence, much to the amusement of his young friends. Mr. Crackit took up his hat to go.

'Has nobody been, Toby?' asked Fagin.

'Not a living leg,' answered Mr. Crackit, pulling up his collar; 'it's been as dull as swipes. You ought to stand something handsome, Fagin, to recompense me for keeping house for so long.

'Dodger! Charley!' cried Fagin, 'it's time you were on the lay. Come! It's near ten and nothing done yet.' When they had left the room Fagin continued: 'Now, I'll go and get you that cash, Nancy. This is only the key of a little cupboard where I keep a few odd things the boys get, my dear. I never lock up my money, for I've got none to lock up, my dear—ha, ha, ha—none to lock up. Hush!' he said, hastily concealing the key in his breast; 'who's that? Listen!'

The girl, who was sitting at the table with her arms folded, appeared in no way interested in the arrival or to care whether the person, whoever he was, came or went, until the murmur of a man's voice reached her ears. The instant she caught the sound she tore off her bonnet and shawl, with the rapidity of lightning, and thrust them under the table. The Jew, turning round immediately afterwards, she muttered a complaint of the heat in a tone of languor that contrasted very remarkably with the extreme haste and violence of this action, which, however, had been unobserved by Fagin, who had his back towards her at the time.

'Bah!' he whispered, as though nettled by the interruption; 'it's the man I expected before; he's coming downstairs. Not a word about the money while he's here, Nance. He won't stop long. Not ten minutes, my dear.'

Laying a skinny forefinger upon his lip, the Jew carried a candle to the door, as a man's step was heard upon the step without. He reached it at the same moment as the visitor, who, coming hastily into the room, was close upon the girl before he observed her.

It was Monks.

'Only one of my young people,' said Fagin, observing that Monks drew back on beholding a stranger. 'Don't move, Nancy.'

The girl drew closer to the table and, glancing at Monks with an air of careless levity, withdrew her eyes, but as he turned his towards Fagin, she stole another look so keen and searching, and full of purpose, that if there had been any by-stander to observe the change, he could hardly have believed the two looks to have proceeded from the same person.

'Any news?' inquired Fagin.

'Great.'

'And—and—good?' asked Fagin, hesitating as though he feared to vex the other man by being too sanguine.

'Not bad, anyway,' replied Monks with a smile.

The Jew pointed upwards and took Monks out of the room. Slipping off her shoes, Nancy followed and stood at the door, listening with breathless interest. When Fagin returned, after Monks had gone off into the street, the girl was adjusting her shawl and bonnet, as if preparing to be gone.

'Why, Nance,' exclaimed the Jew, starting back as he put down the candle. 'how pale you are! What have you been doing to yourself?'

'Nothing that I know of except sitting in this close place, for I don't know how long and all,' replied the girl carelessly. 'Come! Let me get back; that's a dear.'

With a sigh for every piece of money, Fagin counted the amount into her hand. They parted without more conversation, merely interchanging a 'goodnight'.

If Nancy betrayed any agitation when she presented herself to Mr. Sikes, he did not observe it; for merely inquiring if she had brought the money, and receiving a reply in the affirmative, he uttered a growl of satisfaction, and replacing his head upon the pillow, resumed the slumbers which her arrival had interrupted.

It was fortunate for her that the possession of money occasioned him so much employment next day in the way of eating and drinking, and withal had so beneficial an effect in smoothing down the asperities of his temper that he had neither time nor inclination to be very critical upon her behaviour and deportment. That she had all the abstracted and nervous manner of one who is on the eve of some bold and hazardous step, which it has required no common struggle to resolve upon, would have been obvious to the lynx-eyed Fagin.

When night came on, she sat by watching until the house-breaker, with many grumbling oaths, called for his physic. Then she jumped up with great alacrity, poured it out quickly but with her back towards him, and held the vessel to his lips while he drank of the contents. Two or three minutes later his arm fell languidly by his side, and he lay like one in a profound trance.

'The laudanum has taken effect at last,' murmured the girl as she rose from the bedside. 'I may be too late even now.'

She hastily dressed in her bonnet and shawl, looking fearfully round from time to time as if, despite the sleeping draught, she expected every moment to feel the pressure of Sikes's heavy hand upon her shoulder; then, stooping softly over the bed, she kissed the robber's lips, and, opening and closing the room door with noiseless touch, hurried from the house.

A watchman was crying half-past nine down a dark passage through which she had to pass in gaining the main thorough-fare.

'Has it long gone the half-hour?' asked the girl.

'It'll strike the hour in another quarter,' said the man, raising his lantern to her face.

'And I cannot get there in less than an hour or more,' muttered Nancy, brushing swiftly past him and gliding rapidly down the street.

Many of the shops were already closing in the back lanes and avenues through which she tracked her way, in making from Spitalfields towards the West End of London. The clock struck ten, increasing her impatience, and she tore along the narrow pavement until she reached the more wealthy quarter of the town where she found her destination.

It was a family hotel in a quiet but handsome street near Hyde Park. As the brilliant light of the lamp, which burnt before its door, guided her to the spot, the clock struck eleven. She had loitered for a few paces as though irresolute

and making up her mind to advance; but the sound determined her and she stepped into the hall. The porter's seat was
vacant. She looked round with an air of incertitude and
advanced towards the stairs.

'Now, young woman!' said a smartly dressed female,
looking out from a door behind her, 'who do you want
here?'

'A lady who is stopping in this house,' answered the girl.

'A lady!' was the reply, accompanied with a scornful look.
'What lady?'

'Miss Maylie,' said Nancy.

The young woman, who had by this time noted her
appearance, replied only by a look of virtuous disdain, and
summoned a man to answer her. To him Nancy repeated her
request.

'What name am I to say?' asked the waiter.

'It's of no use saying any,' replied Nancy. 'Just say that a
young woman earnestly asks to speak to Miss Maylie alone.'

The man ran upstairs. Nancy remained, pale and almost
breathless, until the man returned and said the young woman
was to walk upstairs.

Nancy followed the man with trembling limbs, to a small
antechamber lighted by a lamp from the ceiling. Here he left
her and retired. When she heard a light step approaching
the door opposite to that by which she had entered, she
raised her eyes sufficiently to observe that the figure which
presented itself was that of a slight and beautiful girl; then
bending them on the ground, she tossed her head with
affected carelessness as she said:

'It's a hard matter to get to see you, lady. If I had taken
offence and gone away, as many would have done, you'd
have been sorry for it one day, and not without reason
either.'

'I am very sorry if anyone has behaved harshly to you,'
replied Rose. 'Do not think of that. Tell me why you wished
to see me. I am the person you enquired for.'

At the kind tone of this answer Nancy burst into tears.

'Sit down,' said Rose earnestly. 'If you are in poverty or
affliction I shall be truly glad to relieve you if I can—I shall
indeed. Sit down.'

'Let me stand, lady,' said the girl, still weeping, 'and do not speak to me so kindly until you know me better. It is growing late. Is—is—that door shut?'

'Yes,' said Rose, recoiling a few steps, as if to be nearer assistance in case she should require it. 'Why?'

'Because,' said the girl, 'I am about to put my life and the lives of others in your hands. I am the girl that dragged little Oliver back to old Fagin's, on the night he went out from the house in Pentonville.'

'You!' said Rose Maylie.

'I, lady,' replied the girl. 'I am the infamous creature you have heard of that lives among the thieves. But I have stolen away from those who would surely murder me, if they knew I had been here, to tell you what I have overheard. Do you know a man named Monks?'

'No,' said Rose.

'He knows you,' replied the girl, 'and knew you were here, for it was by hearing him tell the place that I found you out.'

'I never heard the name,' said Rose.

'Then he goes by some other amongst us,' rejoined the girl, 'which I more than thought before. Some time ago, and soon after Oliver was put into your house on the night of the robbery, I—suspecting this man—listened to a conversation held between him and Fagin in the dark. I found out, from what I heard, that Monks—the man I asked you about, you know——'

'Yes,' said Rose, 'I understand.'

'... that Monks,' pursued the girl, 'had seen him accidentally with two of our boys on the day we first lost him, and had known him directly to be the same child he was watching for, though I couldn't make out why. A bargain was struck with Fagin, that if Oliver was got back he would have a certain sum; and he was to have more for making him a thief, which this Monks wanted for some purpose of his own.'

'For what purpose?' asked Rose.

'He caught sight of my shadow on the wall as I listened, in the hope of finding out,' said the girl, 'so I heard no more and I saw him no more till last night.'

'And what occurred then?'

'I'll tell you, lady. Last night he came again. Again they went upstairs, and I, wrapping myself up so that my shadow should not betray me, again listened at the door. The first words I heard Monks say were these: 'So the only proofs of the boy's identity lie at the bottom of the river, and the old hag that received them from the mother is rotting in her coffin.' They laughed, and talked of his success in doing this; and Monks, talking on about the boy and getting very wild, said that though he had got the young devil's money safely now, he'd rather have had it the other way; for what a game it would have been to have brought down the boast of the father's will, by driving him through every jail in town, and then hauling him up for some capital felony which Fagin could easily manage, after having made a good profit of him besides.'

'What is all this?' said Rose.

'The truth, lady, though it comes from my lips,' replied the girl. 'Then, he said, with oaths common enough in my ears, but strange to yours, that if he could gratify his hatred by taking the boy's life without bringing his own neck in danger, he would; but, as he couldn't, he'd be on the watch to meet him at every turn in life; and if he took advantage of his birth and history, he might harm him yet. "In short, Fagin," he says, "Jew as you are, you never laid such snares as I'll contrive for my young brother Oliver." '

'His brother!' exclaimed Rose.

'Those were his words,' said Nancy, glancing uneasily around as she had scarcely ceased to do since she began to speak, for a vision of Sikes haunted her perpetually. 'And more. When he spoke of you and the other lady, and said it seemed contrived by Heaven or the devil against him, that Oliver should come into your hands, he laughed, and said there was some comfort in that too, for how many thousands and hundreds of thousands of pounds would you not give, if you had them, to know who your two-legged spaniel was.'

'You do not mean,' said Rose, turning very pale, 'to tell me that this was said in earnest?'

'He spoke in hard and angry earnest, if a man ever did,' replied the girl, shaking her head. 'He is an earnest man when his hatred is up. I know many who do worse things, but I'd rather listen to them all a dozen times than to that Monks once. It is growing late and I have to reach home without suspicion of having been on such an errand as this. I must get back quickly.'

'But what can I do?' said Rose. 'To what use can I turn this communication without you? Back! Why do you wish to return to companions you paint in such terrible colours? If you repeat this information to a gentleman whom I can summon in an instant from the next room, you can be consigned to some place of safety without half-an-hour's delay.'

'I must go back because—because among the men I have told you of, there is one, the most desperate among them all, that I can't leave—no, not even to be saved from the life I am leading now.'

'It is madness,' cried Rose.

'I don't know what it is,' answered the girl, 'but I am drawn back to him through every suffering and ill-usage.'

'But when can I find you again when it is necessary?' asked Rose.

'Every Sunday night from eleven until the clock strikes twelve,' said the girl without hesitation, 'I will walk on London Bridge if I am alive. And now, God bless you, sweet lady, and send as much happiness on your head as I brought shame on mine!'

Thus speaking, and sobbing aloud, the unhappy creature turned away.

Rose's situation was, indeed, one of no common trial and difficulty. While she felt the most eager and burning desire to penetrate the mystery in which Oliver's history was enveloped, she could not but hold sacred the confidence which the miserable woman with whom she had just conversed had reposed in her as a young and guileless girl.

They purposed remaining in London only three days, prior to departing for some weeks to a distant part of the coast. It was now midnight of the first day. What course of action could she determine upon, which could be adopted in eight-and-forty hours? Or how could she postpone the journey without exciting suspicion?

Mr. Losberne was with them and would be for the next

two days; but Rose was too well acquainted with the excellent gentleman's impetuosity to trust him with the secret. She passed a sleepless and anxious night. After more communing with herself next day, she arrived at the desperate conclusion of consulting Harry.

She had taken up her pen and laid it down again fifty times, and had considered and reconsidered the first line of her letter without writing the first word, when Oliver, who had been walking in the streets, with Mr. Giles as a bodyguard, entered the room in such breathless haste and violent agitation, as seemed to betoken some new cause of alarm.

'What makes you look so flurried?' asked Rose, advancing to meet him.

'I hardly know how: I feel as if I should be choked,' replied the boy. 'Oh dear! To think that I should see him at last, and you should be able to know that I have told you all the truth!'

'I never thought that you had told us anything but the truth,' said Rose, soothing him. 'But what is this?—of whom do you speak?'

'I have seen the gentleman,' replied Oliver, scarcely able to articulate, 'the gentleman who was so good to me—Mr. Brownlow, that we have so often talked about.'

'Where!' asked Rose.

'Getting out of a coach,' replied Oliver, shedding tears of delight, 'and going into a house. Here is the address.'

With her attention not a little distracted by these and a great many other incoherent exclamations of joy, Rose read the address, which was Craven Street in the Strand. She very soon determined upon turning the discovery to account.

'Quick!' she said. 'Tell them to fetch a hackney coach and be ready to go with me. I will take you there directly without a minute's loss of time. I will only tell my aunt that we are going out for an hour, and be ready as soon as you are.'

Oliver needed no prompting to despatch and in little more than five minutes they were on their way to Craven Street. When they arrived there Rose left Oliver in the coach, under pretence of preparing the old gentleman to receive him; and sending up her card by the servant requested to see Mr. Brownlow on very pressing business. The servant soon returned, to beg that she would walk upstairs; and following him into an upper room, Miss Maylie was presented to an elderly gentleman of benevolent appearance, in a bottle-green coat. At no great distance from whom was seated another old gentleman in nankeen breeches and gaiters, who did not look particularly benevolent, and who was sitting with his hands clasped on the top of a thick stick, and his chin propped thereupon.

'Dear me,' said the gentleman in the bottle-green coat, hastily rising with great politeness. 'I beg your pardon, young lady—I imagined it was some importunate person who—I beg you will excuse me. Be seated, pray.'

'Mr. Brownlow, I believe?' said Rose, glancing from the other gentleman to the one who had spoken.

'That is my name,' said the old gentleman. 'This is my friend, Mr. Grimwig. Grimwig, will you leave us for a few minutes.'

'I believe,' interposed Miss Maylie, 'that at this period of our interview, I need not give that gentleman the trouble of going away. If I am correctly informed he is cognizant of the business on which I wish to speak to you. I shall surprise you very much, I have no doubt,' said Rose, naturally em-barrassed, 'but you once showed great benevolence and goodness to a very dear young friend of mine, and I am sure you will take an interest in hearing of him again.'

'Indeed!' said Mr. Brownlow.

'Oliver Twist, you knew him as,' replied Rose.

The words no sooner escaped her lips than Mr. Grimwig, who had been affecting to dip into a large book that lay on the table, upset it with a great crash.

Mr. Brownlow was no less surprised, although his astonish-ment was not expressed in the same eccentric manner. He drew his chair nearer to Miss Maylie's and said:

'If you have it in your power to produce any evidence which will alter the unfavourable opinion I was once induced to entertain of that poor child, in Heaven's name put me in possession of it!'

'A bad one! I'll eat my head if he is not a bad one,' growled Mr. Grimwig, speaking by some ventriloquial power, with-out moving a muscle of his face.

'He is a child of a noble nature and a warm heart,' said Rose colouring; 'and that Power which has thought fit to try him beyond his years, has planted in his breast affections and feelings which would do honour, to many who have numbered his days six times over.'

'Now, Miss Maylie,' said Mr. Brownlow, 'will you let me know what intelligence you have of this poor child, allowing me to promise that I exhausted every means in my power of discovering him, and that since I have been absent from this country, my first impression that he imposed upon me and had been persuaded by his former associates to rob me, has been considerably shaken.'

Rose, who had had time to collect her thoughts, at once related in a few natural words all that had befallen Oliver since he had left Mr. Brownlow's house; reserving Nancy's information for that gentleman's private ear, and concluding that his only sorrow for some months past had been the not being able to meet with his former benefactor and friend.

'Thank God!' said the old gentleman. 'This is great happiness to me, great happiness. But you have not told me where he is, Miss Maylie. You must pardon my finding fault with you—but why not have brought him?'

'He is waiting in a coach at the door,' replied Rose.

'At this door!' cried the old gentleman. With which he hurried out of the room, down the stairs, up the coach steps, and into the coach, without another word.

Mr. Brownlow soon returned accompanied by Oliver, whom Mr. Grimwig received very graciously; and if the gratification of that moment had been the only reward for all her anxiety and care in Oliver's behalf, Rose Maylie would have been well repaid.

'There is somebody else who should not be forgotten, by the by,' said Mr. Brownlow, ringing the bell. 'Send Mrs. Bedwin here, if you please.'

The old housekeeper answered the summons with all dispatch and began to rummage in her pocket for her spectacles. But Oliver's patience was not proof against this new trial; and yielding to his first impulse he sprang into her arms.

'God be good to me!' cried the old lady, embracing him. 'It is my innocent boy!'

'My dear old nurse!' cried Oliver.

'He would come back—I knew he would,' said the old lady, holding him in her arms. 'How well he looks, and how like a gentleman's son he is dressed again! Where have you been this long, long while?'

Leaving her and Oliver to compare notes at leisure, Mr. Brownlow led the way into another room; and there heard from Rose a full narration of her interview with Nancy, which occasioned him no little surprise and perplexity. Rose also explained her reasons for not confiding in her friend Mr. Losberne in the first instance. The old gentleman considered that she had acted prudently and readily undertook to hold solemn conference with the worthy doctor himself. To afford him an early execution of this design it was arranged that he should call at the hotel at eight o'clock that evening and that in the meantime Mrs. Maylie should be cautiously informed of all that had occurred. These preliminaries adjusted, Rose and Oliver returned home.

Rose had by no means overrated the measure of the good doctor's wrath.

'What the devil is to be done?' said the impetuous doctor, when they had rejoined the two ladies. 'Are we to pass a vote of thanks to all these vagabonds, male and female, and beg them accept a hundred pounds or so apiece, as a trifling mark of our esteem, and some slight acknowledgement of their kindness to Oliver?'

'Not exactly that,' returned Mr. Brownlow, laughing, 'but we must proceed gently and with great care. It is quite clear that we shall have extreme difficulty in getting to the bottom of this mystery, unless we can bring this man Monks upon his knees. That can only be done by stratagem, and by catching him when he is not surrounded by these people. For, suppose he were apprehended, we have no proof against him. He is not even (so far as we know, or as the facts appear to us) concerned with the gang in any of their robberies. If he were not discharged, it is very unlikely that he could receive any further punishment than being committed to prison as a rogue and vagabond; and of course, ever afterwards his mouth would be so obstinately closed that he might as well, for our purposes, be deaf, dumb, blind, and an idiot. But before we can resolve upon any precise course of action, it will be necessary to see the girl, to ascertain from her whether she will point out this Monks, on the understanding that he is to be dealt with by us, and not by the law; or, if she will not, to procure from her such an account of his haunts and description of his person as will enable us to identify him. She cannot be seen until next Sunday night; this is Tuesday. I would suggest that in the meantime we remain perfectly quiet, and keep these matters secret.'

'I should like,' he continued, 'to call in the aid of my friend Grimwig. He is a strange creature, but a shrewd one, and might prove of material assistance to us; I should say he was bred a lawyer and quitted the Bar in disgust because he had only one brief and a motion of course in twenty years, though whether that is a recommendation or not, you must determine for yourselves.'

'I have no objection to your calling in your friend if I may call in mine,' said the doctor.

'We must put it to the vote,' said Mr. Brownlow. 'Who may he be?'

'That lady's son, and this young lady's—very old friend,' said the doctor motioning towards Mrs. Maylie and concluding with an expressive glance at her niece.

Rose blushed deeply, but she did not make any audible objection to this motion (possibly she felt in a hopeless minority); and Harry Maylie and Mr. Grimwig were accordingly added to the committee.

'We stay in town, of course,' said Mrs. Maylie, 'while there remains the slightest prospect of prosecuting this inquiry with a chance of success.'

'Good!' rejoined Mr. Brownlow. 'And as I see on the faces about me a disposition to inquire how it happened that I was not in the way to corroborate Oliver's tale, and had so suddenly left the kingdom, let me stipulate that I shall be asked no questions until such time as I may deem it expedient to forestall them by telling my own story. Come! Supper has been announced, and young Oliver, who is all alone in the next room, will have begun to think, by this time, that we have wearied of his company and entered into some dark conspiracy to thrust him forth upon the world.'

With these words the old gentleman gave his hand to Mrs. Maylie and escorted her into the supper room. Mr. Losberne followed, leading Rose; and the council was, for the present, effectually broken up.

II

NANCY PAYS FOR HER HELP

Upon the night when Nancy, having lulled Mr. Sikes to sleep, hurried on her self-imposed mission to Rose Maylie, there advanced towards London by the Great North Road two persons upon whom it is expedient that this history should bestow some attention.

They were a man and a woman. The former was one of those long limbed, knock-kneed, shambling bony people to whom it is difficult to assign any precise age. The woman was young but of robust and hardy make; as she need have been to bear the weight of the heavy bundle which was strapped to her back. Her companion was not encumbered with much luggage as there merely dangled from a stick, which he carried over his shoulder, a small parcel wrapped in a common handkerchief, and apparently light enough.

Thus they had toiled along the dusty road, taking little heed of any object in sight, save when they stepped aside to allow a wider passage for the mail-coaches which were whirling out of town, until they passed through Highgate Archway, when the foremost traveller stopped and called impatiently to his companion.

'Come on, can't yer? What a lazybones yer are, Charlotte.'

'Is it much farther?' asked the woman resting herself against a bank and looking up with the perspiration streaming from her face.

'Much farther! Yer as good as there,' said the long-legged tramper pointing before him. 'Look there! Those are the lights of London.'

'They're a good two mile off, at least,' said the woman despondingly.

'Never mind whether they're two mile off or twenty,' said Noah Claypole, for he it was, 'but get up and come on, or I'll kick yer, and so I give yer notice.'

As Noah's red nose grew redder with anger, and as he crossed the road while speaking, as if fully prepared to put his threat into execution, the woman rose without any further remark and trudged onward by his side.

'Where do you mean to stop for the night, Noah?' she asked after they had walked a few hundred yards.

'How should I know?' replied Noah, whose temper had been considerably impaired by walking.

'Near, I hope,' said Charlotte.

'No, not near,' replied Mr. Claypole. 'A pretty thing it would be, wouldn't it, to go and stop at the very first public house outside the town, so that Sowerberry, if he come up after us, might poke in his nose and have us taken back in a cart with handcuffs on,' said Mr. Claypole in a jeering tone. 'No! I shall go and lose myself among the narrowest streets I can find, and not stop until we come to the very out-of-the-wayest house I can set eyes on. 'Cod, yer may thank yer stars I've got a head; for if we hadn't gone, at first, the wrong road a purpose, and come back across country, yer'd have been locked up hard and fast a week ago, my lady. And serve yer right for being a fool.'

'I know I ain't as cunning as you are,' replied Charlotte, 'but don't put all the blame on me and say *I* should have been locked up. You would have been if I had been any-way.'

'Yer took the money from the till, yer know yer did,' said Mr. Claypole.

'I took it for you, Noah dear,' rejoined Charlotte.

'Did I keep it?' asked Mr. Claypole.

'No, you trusted in me and let me carry it, like a dear, and so you are,' said the lady, chuckling him under the chin, and drawing her arm through his.

Mr. Claypole went on without halting until he arrived at the Angel at Islington, where he wisely judged from the crowd of passengers and number of vehicles that London began in earnest. Just pausing to observe which appeared the most crowded streets and consequently the most to be avoided, he crossed into St. John's Road and was soon deep in the obscurity of the intricate and dirty ways which, lying between Gray's Inn Lane and Smithfield, render that part of the town one of the lowest and worst that improvement has left in the midst of London.

Through these streets Noah Claypole walked, dragging Charlotte after him. At length he stopped in front of one more humble in appearance and more dirty than any he had yet seen, and graciously announced his intention of putting up there for the night.

'So give us the bundle,' said Noah, unstrapping it from the woman's shoulders and slinging it over his own; 'and don't yer speak except when yer spoke to. What's the name of the house—t-h-r—three what?'

'Cripples,' said Charlotte.

'Three Cripples,' repeated Noah, 'and a very good sign too. Now then! Keep close at my heels and come along.' With these injunctions he pushed the rattling door with his shoulder and entered the house, followed by his companion.

There was nobody in the bar but a young Jew, who, with his two elbows on the counter, was reading a dirty newspaper.

'Is this the Three Cripples?' asked Noah.

'That is the dabe of this 'ouse,' replied the Jew.

'A gentleman we met on the road, coming up from the country, recommended us here,' said Noah, nudging Charlotte perhaps to call her attention for this most ingenious device for attracting respect and perhaps to warn her to betray no surprise. 'We want to sleep here tonight.'

'I'b dot certaid you cad,' said Barney, who was the attendant sprite, 'but I'll idquire.'

'Show us the tap and give us a bit of cold meat and a drop of beer while yer inquiring, will yer?' said Noah.

Barney complied by ushering them into a small back room and setting the viands before them, having done which, he informed the travellers that they could be lodged that night and left the amiable couple to their refreshment. Now this back room was immediately behind the bar and some steps lower, so that any person connected with the house, undrawing a small curtain which concealed a single pane of glass fixed in the wall between, could not only look down into the back-room but ascertain with tolerable distinctness their subject of conversation. Barney had only just returned when Fagin, in the course of his evening's business, came into the bar to inquire after some of his young pupils.

'Hush,' said Barney, 'stradgers id the next room.'

'Strangers!' repeated the old man in a whisper.

'Ah! Ad rub uds too,' added Barney. 'Frob the cuttry, but subthing in your way, or I'b bistaked.'

Fagin appeared to receive this communication with great interest. Mounting a stool, he cautiously applied his eye to the pane of glass, and turning his ear to the partition listened attentively, with a subtle and eager look upon his face, that might have appertained to some old goblin.

'So I mean to be a gentleman,' said Mr. Claypole, kicking out his legs and continuing a conversation the commencement of which Fagin had arrived too late to hear. 'No more jolly old coffins, Charlotte, but a gentlemen's life for me; and if yer like, yer shall be a lady.'

'I should like that well enough, dear,' replied Charlotte, 'but tills ain't to be emptied every day, and people to get clear off after it.'

'Tills be blowed!' said Mr. Claypole, 'There's more things besides tills to be emptied.'

'What do you mean?' asked his companion.

'Pockets, women's ridicules, houses, mail coaches, banks!' said Mr. Claypole rising with the porter.

'But you can't do all that, dear,' said Charlotte.

'I shall look out to get into company with them as can,' replied Noah. 'They'll be able to make us useful some way or another. Why, you yourself are worth fifty women; I never see such a precious sly and deceitful creetur as yer can be when I let yer.'

'Lor, how nice it is to hear you say so!' exclaimed Charlotte, imprinting a kiss upon his ugly face. The sudden opening of the door and the appearance of a stranger, interrupted her.

The stranger was Mr. Fagin. And very amiable he looked, and a very low bow he made, as he advanced, and setting himself down at the nearest table, ordered something to drink of the grinning Barney.

'A pleasant night, sir, but cool for the time of year,' said Fagin rubbing his hands. 'From the country, I see, sir?'

'How do yer see that?' asked Noah Claypole.

'We have not so much dust as that in London,' replied Fagin, pointing from Noah's shoes to those of his companion and from them to the two bundles.

'Yer a sharp feller,' said Noah. 'Ha! ha! Only hear that, Charlotte!'

'Why, one need be sharp in this town, my dear,' replied the Jew, sinking his voice to a confidential whisper. 'A man need be always emptying a till, or a pocket, or a woman's reticule, or a mail-coach, or a bank, if he drinks regularly.'

Mr. Claypole no sooner heard this extract from his own remarks than he fell back in his chair, and looked from the Jew to Charlotte with a countenance of ashy paleness and excessive terror.

'Don't mind me, my dear,' said Fagin, drawing his chair closer. 'Ha! ha! It was lucky it was only me who heard you by chance. It was very lucky it was only me.'

'I didn't take it,' stammered Noah, no longer stretching out his legs like an independent gentleman, but coiling them up as well as he could up under his chair; 'it was all her doing; yer've got it now, Charlotte, yer know yer have.'

'No matter who's got or who did it, my dear,' replied Fagin, glancing nevertheless, with a hawk's eye at the girl and the two bundles. 'I'm in that way myself, and I like you for it.'

'In what way?' asked Mr. Claypole, a little recovering.

'In that way of business,' rejoined Fagin, 'and so are the people of the house. You've hit the right nail upon the head, and are as safe here as you could be. There is not a safer place in all this town than is the Cripples; that is, when I like to make it so. And I've taken a fancy to you and the young woman. I've got a friend that I think I can gratify your darling wish and put you, in the right way, where you can take whatever department of the business you think will suit you best.'

'Yer speak as if yer were in earnest,' replied Noah.

'What advantage would it be to me to be anything else?' inquired Fagin, shrugging his shoulders. 'Here! Let me have a word with you outside.'

'There's no occasion to trouble ourselves to move,' said Noah, getting his legs by gradual degrees abroad again.

'She'll take the luggage upstairs the while. Charlotte, see to them bundles!'

This mandate, which had been delivered with great majesty, was obeyed without the slightest demur, and Charlotte made the best of her way off with the packages while Noah held the door open and watched her out.

'She's kept tolerably under, ain't she?' he asked as he resumed his seat, in the tone of a keeper who has tamed some wild animal.

'Quite perfect,' rejoined Fagin, clapping him on the shoulder. 'You're a genius, my dear.'

'Why, I suppose if I wasn't I shouldn't be here,' replied Noah. 'But, I say, she'll be back if yer lose time.'

'Now, what do you think?' said Fagin. 'If you was to like my friend, could you do better than join him?'

'Is he in a good way of business; that's where it is!' responded Noah, winking one of his little eyes.

'The top of the tree, employs a power of hands, has the very best society in the profession.'

'Regular town-maders?' asked Mr. Claypole.

'Not a countryman among 'em; and I don't think he'd take you, even on my recommendation, if he didn't run rather short of assistants just now,' replied Fagin.

'Should I have to hand over?' said Noah, slapping his breeches pocket.

'It couldn't possibly be done without,' replied Fagin, in a most decided manner.

'Twenty pound, though—it's a lot of money!'

'Not when it's in a note you can't get rid of,' retorted Fagin. 'Number and date taken, I suppose? Payment stopped at the Bank? Ah! It's not worth much to him. It'll have to go abroad and he couldn't sell it for a great deal in the market.'

'When could I see him?' asked Noah doubtfully.

'Tomorrow morning.'

'Where?'

'Here?'

'Um!' said Noah. 'What's the wages?'

'Live like a gentleman—board and lodging, pipes and spirits free—half of all you earn, and half of all the young woman earns,' replied Mr. Fagin.

Whether Noah Claypole, whose rapacity was none the least comprehensive, would have acceded to even those glowing terms had he been a perfectly free agent, is very doubtful; but as he recollected that in the event of his refusal it was in the power of his new acquaintance to give him up to justice immediately (and more unlikely things had come to pass), he gradually relented, and said he thought that would suit him.

'But yer see,' observed Noah, 'as she will be able to do a good deal, I should like to take something very light. Something not too trying for the strength, and not very dangerous.'

'The kinchin lay!' said Fagin, laying his hand on Noah's knee.

'What's that?' demanded Mr. Claypole.

'The kinchins, my dear, is the young children that's sent on errands by their mothers, with sixpences and shillings, and lay is just to take their money away, then knock 'em into the kennel and walk off very slow. Ha! Ha! Ha!

'Ha! Ha!' roared Mr. Claypole. 'Lord, that's the very thing!'

Next day Noah and Charlotte removed to the Jew's house.

'So it was you that was your own friend?' asked Mr. Claypole. ''Cod, I thought as much last night!'

'Every man's his own friend, my dear,' replied Fagin. 'But don't forget, to keep my little business all snug, you depend upon me and I depend upon you. It's this mutual trust we have in each other that consoles me under heavy losses. My best hand was taken from me yesterday morning. He was wanted.'

'Very particular?' inquired Mr. Claypole—or Mr. Morris Bolter, to use the name he had given to the Jew on the previous evening.

'No,' replied Fagin, 'not very. He was charged with attempting to pick a pocket, and they found a silver snuff-box on him—his own, my dear, his own, for he took snuff himself, and was very fond of it. They remanded him till today, for they thought they knew the owner. Ah! He was worth fifty boxes, and I'd give the price of as many to have him back. You should have known the Dodger, my dear, you should have known the Dodger.'

'Well, but I shall know him, I hope; don't yer think so?' said Mr. Bolter.

'I'm doubtful about it,' replied Fagin with a sigh. 'If they don't get any fresh evidence, it'll only be a summary conviction, and we shall have him back again after six weeks or so; but if they do, it's a case of lagging. They know what a clever lad he is; he'll be a lifer. They'll make the Artful nothing less than a lifer.'

'What do yer mean by lagging and a lifer?' demanded Mr. Bolter. 'What's the good of talking in that way to me? Why don't yer speak so I can understand yer?'

Fagin was about to translate these mysterious expressions into the vulgar tongue; and, being interpreted, Mr. Bolter would have been informed that they represented that combination of words, 'transportation for life', when the dialogue was cut short by the entry of Master Bates, with his hands in his breeches' pockets and his face twisted into a look of semi-comical woe.

'It's all up, Fagin,' said Charley, when he and his new companion had been made known to each other.

'What do you mean?'

'They've found the gentleman as owns the box; two or three more's a-coming to identify him; and the Artful's booked for a passage out,' replied Master Bates. 'I must have a full suit of mourning, Fagin, and a hatband, to wisit him in, afore he sets out upon his travels. To think of Jack Dawkins—lummy Jack—the Dodger—the Artful Dodger—going abroad for a common twopenny-halfpenny sneeze-box!'

'Never mind, Charley,' said Fagin soothingly; 'it'll come out. They'll all know what a clever fellow he was; and he'll show it himself, and not disgrace his old pals and teachers. Think how young he is too! What a distinction, Charley, to be lagged at his time of life!'

* * * *

Adept as she was in all the arts of cunning and dissimulation, the girl Nancy could not wholly conceal the effect which the knowledge of the step she had taken wrought upon her mind.

It was Sunday night, and the bell of the nearest church struck the hour. Sikes and the Jew were talking but they paused to listen. The girl looked up from the low seat on whch she crouched, and listened too. Eleven.

'An hour this side of midnight,' said Sikes, raising the blind to look out and returning to his seat. 'Dark and heavy it is too. A good night for business, this.'

'Ah!' replied Fagin. 'What a pity, Bill my dear, that there's none quite ready to be done.'

'You're right for once,' replied Sikes gruffly. 'It is a pity for I'm in the humour too.'

Fagin offered no reply, but pulling Sikes by the sleeve, pointed his finger towards Nancy, who had taken advantage of the foregoing conversation to put on her bonnet and was now leaving the room.

'Hallo,' cried Sikes, 'Nance. Where's the gal going at this time of night?'

'I don't know where,' replied the girl.

'Then I do,' said Sikes, more in the spirit of obstinacy than because he had any real objection to the girl going where she listed. 'Nowhere. Sit down.'

'I'm not well. I told you that before,' rejoined the girl. 'I want a breath of air.'

'Put your head out of the winder,' replied Sikes.

'There's not enough there,' said the girl. 'I want it in the street.'

'Then you won't have it,' replied Sikes. With which assurance he rose, locked the door, took the key out, and pulling her bonnet from her head, flung it to the top of an old press. 'There,' said the robber. 'Now stop quietly where you are, will you?' And he seized her by the wrist.

'Let me go' screamed the girl. Sikes looked on for a minute, watching his opportunity, and suddenly pinioning her hands dragged her, struggling and wrestling with him by the way into a small room adjoining, where he sat himself on a bench and thrusting her into a chair, held her down by force. She struggled and implored by turns until twelve o'clock had struck, and then, wearied and exhausted, ceased to contest the point any longer. With a caution, backed by many oaths, to make no more efforts to go out that night, Sikes left her to recover at leisure and rejoined Fagin.

'Whew!' said the housebreaker, wiping the perspiration from his face. 'Wot a precious strange gal that is!'

'You may say that, Bill,' replied Fagin thoughtfully. 'You may say that.'

'What did she take it into her head to go out tonight for, do you think?' asked Sikes. 'Come, you should know her better than me. Wot does it mean?'

'Obstinacy; woman's obstinacy, I suppose, my dear.'

'She was hanging about me all day and night too, when I was stretched on my back; and you, like a black-hearted wolf as you are, kept yourself aloof,' said Sikes. 'We was very poor too, all the time, and I think one way or other it's worried and fretted her; and that being shut up here so long has made her restless—eh?'

'That's it, my dear,' replied the Jew in a whisper. 'Hush!'

As he uttered these words the girl herself appeared and resumed her former seat. Her eyes were swollen and red; she rocked herself to and fro, tossed her head, and, after a little time, burst out laughing.

'Why, now she's on the other tack!' exclaimed Sikes, turning a look of excessive surprise on his companion.

Fagin nodded to him to take no further notice just then; and, in a few minutes, the girl subsided into her accustomed demeanour. Whispering to Sikes that there was no fear of her relapsing, Fagin took up his hat and bid him goodnight. He paused when he reached the room door and looking round asked if somebody would light him down the dark stairs.

'Light him down,' said Sikes, who was filling his pipe. 'It's a pity he should break his neck himself and disappoint the sightseers. Show him a light.'

Nancy followed the old man downstairs with a candle. When he reached the passage he laid his finger on his lip and, drawing close to the girl, said in a whisper,

'What is it, Nancy dear? If he is so hard with you (he's a brute, Nance, a brute-beast), why don't you come to me, I say, come to me?'

Nancy shrank back as Fagin offered to lay his hand on hers, but said good-night in a steady voice, and answering his parting look with a nod of intelligence, closed the door between them.

Fagin walked towards his home, intent upon the thoughts that were working within his brain. He had conceived the idea—not from what had just passed, though that had tended to confirm him, but slowly by degrees—that Nancy, wearied of the housebreaker's brutality, had conceived an attachment for some new friend. The object of this new liking was not among his myrmidons. He would be a valuable acquisition with such an assistant as Nancy, and must (thus Fagin argued) be secured without delay.

There was another and a darker object to be gained, Sikes knew too much. 'With a little persuasion,' thought Fagin, 'what more likely than that she would consent to poison him? There would be the dangerous villain gone; another secured in his place; and my influence over the girl unlimited.'

These things passed through the mind of Fagin during the short time he sat alone in the housebreaker's room; and with them uppermost in his thoughts, he had taken the opportunity afterwards afforded him, of sounding the girl in the broken hints he threw out at parting. There was no expression of surprise, no assumption of an inability to understand his meaning. The girl clearly comprehended it. Her glance at parting showed *that*.

The old man was up betimes next morning, and waited impatiently for the appearance of his new associate, who after a delay that seemed interminable, at length presented himself and commenced a voracious assault on the breakfast.

'Bolter,' said Fagin, drawing up a chair and seating himself opposite Morris Bolter.

'Well, here I am,' returned Noah. 'What's the matter? Don't yer ask me to do anything till I have done eating. That's a great fault in this place. Yer never get time enough over yer meals.'

'You can talk as you eat, can't you?' said Fagin, cursing his dear young friend's greediness from the very bottom of his heart.

'Oh yes. I can talk. I get on better when I talk,' said Noah, cutting a monstrous slice of bread. 'Where's Charlotte?'

'Out,' said Fagin. 'I sent her out with the other young woman, because I wanted us to be alone.' Fagin continued: 'You did well yesterday, my dear. Beautiful! The kinchin lay will be a fortune to you.'

'Don't you forget to add three pint pots and a milk can,' said Mr. Bolter.

'No, no, my dear. The pint pots were great strokes of genius: but the milk can was a perfect masterpiece.'

'Pretty well, I think, for a beginner,' remarked Mr. Bolter complacently.

'I want you,' said Fagin, leaning over the table, 'to do a piece of work for me, my dear, that needs great care and caution. It's to dodge a woman for one pound.'

'Who is she?' inquired Noah.

'One of us.'

'Oh lor,' cried Noah, curling up his nose. 'Yer doubtful of her, are yer?'

'She has found out some new friends, my dear, and I must know who they are,' replied Fagin.

'I see,' said Noah. 'Just to have the pleasuer of knowing them, if they're respectable people, eh? Ha! Ha! Ha! I'm your man. Where is she? Where am I to wait for her? Where am I to go?'

'All that my dear, you shall hear from me at the proper time. You keep ready, and leave the rest to me.'

That night, and the next, and the next again, the spy sat booted and equipped in a carter's dress, ready to turn out at a word from Fagin.

Six nights passed, and on each Fagin came home with a disappointed face, and briefly intimated that it was not yet time. On the seventh he returned earlier, and with an exultattion he could not conceal. It was Sunday.

'She goes abroad tonight,' said Fagin, 'and on the right errand, I'm sure; for she has been alone all day, and the man she is afraid of will not be back much before daybreak. Come with me!'

Noah started up without saying a word, for the Jew was in such a state of intense excitement that it infected him. They left the house stealthily and, hurrying through a labyrinth of streets, arrived at length before a public house which Noah recognised as the same in which he had slept on the night of his arrival in London.

It was past eleven o'clock and the door was closed. It opened softly on its hinges as Fagin gave a low whistle. They entered without noise, and the door was closed behind them.

Scarcely venturing to whisper, but substituting dumb-show

for words Fagin and the young Jew who had admitted them pointed out the pane of glass to Noah, and signed to him to climb up and observe the person in the adjoining room.

'Is that the woman?' he asked, scarcely above his breath.

Fagin nodded yes.

Noah looked at her for some time. When she got up and went out, Noah Claypole followed her cautiously.

The church clocks chimed three quarters past eleven as two figures emerged on London Bridge. One which advanced with a swift and rapid step, was that of a woman who looked eagerly about her as though in quest of some expected object; the other figure was that of a man who slunk along in the deepest shadow he could find and, at some distance, accommodated his pace to hers, stopping when she stopped and, when she moved again, creeping stealthily on, but never allowing himself in the ardour of his pursuit, to gain upon her footsteps. At nearly the centre of the bridge, she stopped. The man stopped too.

Midnight had not struck two minutes when a young lady, accompanied by a grey-haired gentleman, alighted from a hackney-carriage within a short distance of the bridge, and having dismissed the vehicle, walked straight towards it. They had scarcely set foot upon its pavement when the girl started and immediately made towards them.

They walked on looking about them with the air of persons who entertained some very slight expectation which had little chance of being realized, when they were suddenly joined by this new associate. They halted with an exclamation of surprise, but suppressed it immediately; for a man in the garments of a countryman came close up—brushed against them, indeed—at that precise moment.

'Not here,' said Nancy hurriedly, 'I am afraid to speak to you here. Come away—out of the public road—down the steps yonder.'

As she uttered these words, and indicated with her hand the direction in which she wished them to proceed, the countryman looked round, and roughly asking what they took up the whole pavement for, passed on.

The steps to which the girl had pointed were those which, on the Surrey bank, and on the same side of the bridge as St.

Saviour's Church, form a landing stage from the river. To this spot the man bearing the appearance of a countryman hastened unobserved; and after a moment's survey of the place he began to descend the lower steps, the tide being out, and hid himself behind a pilaster at the bottom. Suddenly he heard steps near him. He drew himself straight against the wall, and scarcely breathing, listened attentively.

'This is far enough,' said a voice, which was evidently that of the gentleman. 'I will not suffer the young lady to go any farther. Many people would have distrusted you too much to have come even so far, but you see I am willing to humour you.'

'To humour me!' cried the voice of the girl whom he had followed. 'You're considerate indeed, sir. To humour me! Well, well, it's no matter.'

'Why, for what,' said the gentleman in a kinder tone, 'for what purpose can you have brought us to this strange place? Why not have let me speak to you above there, where it is light and there is something stirring, instead of bringing us to this dark and dismal hole?'

'Speak to her kindly,' said the young lady to her companion. 'Poor creature, she seems to need it.'

'You were not here last Sunday night,' the gentleman said. 'I couldn't come,' replied Nancy, 'I was kept by force.' 'By whom?'

'Him that I told the young lady of before.'

'You were not suspected of holding any communication with anybody on the subject which has brought us here tonight, I hope?' asked the old gentleman.

'No,' replied the girl, shaking her head. 'It's not very easy for me to leave him unless he knows why; I couldn't have seen the lady when I did, but that I gave him a drink of laudanum before I came away.'

'Did he awake before you returned?' inquired the gentleman. 'No; and neither he nor any of them suspect me.'

'Good!' said the gentleman, 'Now listen to me.'

'I am ready,' replied the girl, as he paused for a moment.

'This young lady,' the gentleman began, 'has communicated to me and some other friends who can be safely trusted, what you told her nearly a fortnight since. I confess to you that I had doubts at first, whether you were to be implicitly relied upon, but now I firmly believe you are.'

'I am,' said the girl earnestly.

'I repeat that I firmly believe it. To prove to you that I am disposed to trust you, I tell you without reserve, that we propose to extort the secret, whatever it may be, from the fears of this man Monks. But if—if—' said the gentleman, 'he cannot be secured, or, if secured, cannot be acted upon as we wish, you must deliver up the Jew.'

'Fagin!' cried the girl, recoiling.

'That man must be delivered up by you,' said the gentleman.

'I will not do it! I will never do it!' replied the girl. 'Devil that he is, and worse than devil as he has been to me, I will never do that.'

'Tell me why?'

'For one reason,' rejoined the girl firmly, 'for one reason that the lady knows and will stand by me in. I know she will for I have her promise; and for this other reason besides, that, bad life as he has led, I have led a bad life too; there are many of us who have kept the same courses together, and I'll not turn upon them who might—any of them—have turned upon me, but didn't, bad as they are.'

'Then,' said the gentleman, quickly, as if this had been the point he had been aiming to attain, 'put Monks into my hands and leave him to me to deal with.'

'What if he turns against the others?'

'I promise you in that case, if the truth is forced from him, there the matter will rest; there must be circumstances in Oliver's little history which it would be painful to drag before the public eye, and if the truth is once elicited they shall go scot free.'

'And if it is not?' suggested the girl.

'Then,' pursued the gentleman, 'this Fagin shall not be brought to justice without your consent. In such a case I could show you reasons, I think, which would induce you to yield to it.'

'Monks would never learn how you knew what you do?' asked the girl, after a short pause.

'Never,' replied the gentleman.

After receiving an assurance from both that she might

safely take their word, Nancy proceeded in a voice so low,
that it was often difficult for the listener to discover even the
purport of what she said, to describe, by name and situation,
the public house whence she had been followed that night.
When she had thoroughly examined the localities of the
place, the best position from which to watch it without
exciting observation, and the night and hour on which
Monks was most in the habit of frequenting it, she recalled
his features and appearance more forcibly to her recollection.

'He is tall,' said the girl, 'and a strongly made man, but
not stout; he has a lurking walk, and as he walks constantly
looks over his shoulder, first on one side and then on the
other. Don't forget that, for his eyes are sunk in his head so
much deeper than any other man's that you might almost tell
him by that alone. His face is dark like hair and eyes; and
although he can't be more than six- or eight-and-twenty,
withered and haggard. His lips are often discoloured and
disfigured with the marks of teeth; for he has desperate
fits, and sometimes even bites his hands and covers them
with wounds—why did you start?' said the girl, stopping
suddenly.

The gentleman replied, in a hurried manner, that he was
not conscious of having done so, and begged her to proceed.

'Upon his throat, so high that you can see a part of it below
his neckerchief when he turns his face, there is——'

'A broad red mark, like a burn or scald?' cried the gentleman.

'How's this?' said the girl. 'You know him?'

The young lady uttered a cry of surprise, and for a few
moments they were so still that the listener could distinctly
hear them breathe.

'I think I do,' said the gentleman, breaking silence. 'I
should by your description. We shall see. Many people are
singularly like each other. It may not be the same.'

As he expressed himself to this effect, with assumed carelessness, he took a step or two nearer the concealed spy, as the
latter could tell with the distinctness with which he heard him
mutter 'It must be!'

'Now,' he said returning (so it seemed by the sound) to the

spot where he had stood before, 'you have given us most valuable assistance, young woman, and I wish you to be the better for it. What can I do to serve you? Come! I would not have you go back to exchange one word with any old companion, or breathe the very air which is death and pestilence to you. Quit them all while there is time and opportunity.'

'No, sir,' replied Nancy after a short struggle with herself. 'I am chained to my old life. I loathe and hate it now, but I cannot leave it. I must go home.'

'Home!' repeated the young lady, with great stress on the word.

'Home, lady,' rejoined the girl. 'To such a home as I have raised for myself with the work of my whole life. Let us part. I shall be watched or seen. Go! Go! If I have done you any service, all I ask is that you leave me and let me go my way alone. Bless you! God bless you. Good-night, good-night!'

The violent agitation of the girl, and the apprehension of some discovery which would subject her to ill-usage and violence seemed to determine the gentleman to leave her as she requested. The sound of retreating footsteps was audible and the voices ceased.

The two figures of the young lady and her companion soon afterwards appeared upon the bridge. They stopped at the summit of the stairs.

'Hark!' cried the young lady, listening. 'Did she call? I thought I heard her voice.'

'No, my love,' replied Mr. Brownlow, looking sadly back. 'She has not moved, and will not until we are gone.'

As they disappeared the girl sunk down, nearly at her full length upon one of the stone stairs, and vented the anguish of her heart in bitter tears.

After a time she arose, and with feeble and tottering steps ascended to the street. The astonished listener remained motionless at his post for some minutes afterwards and, having ascertained with many cautious glances round him, that he was again alone, crept slowly from his hiding place and returned, stealthily and in the shade of the wall, in the same manner as he had descended.

Peeping out more than once, when he reached the top, to make sure that he was unobserved, Noah Claypole darted

away at his utmost speed, and made for the Jew's house fast
as his legs would carry him.

* * * *

It was nearly two hours before day-break, that time which
in the autumn of the year can be truly called the dead of
night, when the streets are silent and deserted, when even
sounds appear to slumber, and profligacy and riot have
staggered home to dream; it was at this still and silent hour
that Fagin sat watching in his old lair, with face so distorted
and pale, and eyes so red and bloodshot, that he looked less
like a man than like some hideous phantom, moist from the
grave and worried by an evil spirit.

Stretched upon a mattress on the floor lay Noah Claypole,
fast asleep. Fagin's thoughts were busy elsewhere.

Mortification at the overthrow of his notable scheme, hatred
of the girl who had dared to palter with strangers, an utter
distrust of her sincerity in refusing to yield him up, bitter
disappointment at the loss of his revenge on Sikes; the fear
of detection and ruin and death; and a fierce and deadly rage
kindled by all—these were the passionate considerations which,
following close upon each other with rapid and ceaseless whirl,
shot through the brain of Fagin as every evil thought and
blackest purpose lay working at his heart.

The bell rang gently. He crept upstairs to the door and
presently returned accompanied by a man muffled to the chin,
who carried a bundle under one arm. Sitting down and throwing back his outer coat, the man displayed the burly frame of
Sikes.

'There!' he said, laying the bundle on the table. 'Take
care of that and do the most you can with it. It's been trouble
enough to get; I thought I should have been here three hours
ago.'

Fagin laid his hand upon the bundle and locking it in the
cupboard, sat down again without speaking.

'Wot now?' cried Sikes. 'Wot do you look at a man so for?'

Fagin raised his right hand and shook his trembling forefinger in the air, but his passion was so great that the power of
speech was for the moment gone.

'Damme!' said Sikes, feeling in his breast with a look of alarm. 'He's gone mad, I must look to myself here.'

'No, no,' rejoined Fagin, finding his voice. 'It's not—you're not the person, Bill. I've no—no fault to find with you.'

'Oh, you haven't, haven't you?' said Sikes, looking sternly at him, and ostentatiously passing a pistol into a more convenient pocket. 'That's lucky—for one of us. Which one that is, don't matter.'

'I've got that to tell you, Bill,' said Fagin, drawing his chair nearer, 'will make you worse than me.'

'Aye?' returned the robber with an incredulous air. 'Tell away! Look sharp, or Nance will think I'm lost.'

'Lost!' cried Fagin. 'She has pretty well settled that in her own mind already. Suppose that lad that's lying there——'

Sikes turned round to where Noah was sleeping, as if he had not previously observed him. 'Well!' he said, resuming his former position.

'Suppose that lad,' pursued Fagin, 'was to peach—was to blow upon us all—first seeking out the right folks for the purpose, and then having a meeting with 'em in the street to paint our likenesses, described every mark that they might know us by, and the crib where we might be most easily taken. Suppose he was to do all this, and besides to blow upon a plant we've all been in, more or less—of his own fancy; to please his own taste, stealing out at nights to find those most interested against us, and peaching to them. Do you hear me?' cried the Jew, his eyes flashing with rage. 'Suppose he did all this, what then?'

'What then!' replied Sikes with a tremendous oath, 'if he was left alive till I came, I'd grind his skull under the iron heel of my boot into as many grains as there are hairs upon his head.'

'Bolter! Bolter, poor lad!' said Fagin, looking up with an expression of devilish anticipation, and speaking slowly and with marked emphasis. 'He's tired—tired with watching for *her* so long—watching for *her*, Bill.'

'Wot d'ye mean?' asked Sikes, drawing back.

Fagin made no answer, but bending over the sleeper again, hauled him into a sitting posture.

'Tell me that again—once again, just for him to hear,' said the Jew, pointing to Sikes as he spoke.

'Tell yer wot?' asked the sleepy Noah, shaking himself pettishly.

'That about—NANCY,' said Fagin, clutching Sikes by the wrist, as if to prevent his leaving the house before he had heard enough. 'You followed her?'

'Yes.'

'To London Bridge?'

'Yes.'

'Where she met two people?'

'So she did.'

'A gentleman and a lady that she'd gone to of her own accord before, who asked her to give up all her pals, and Monks first—which she did—and to describe him—which she did—and to tell her what house it was that we meet at, and go to—which she did—and where it could be best watched from—which she did—and what time the people, went there, which she did. She did all this. She told it all every word, without a threat, without a murmur—she did— did she not?' cried Fagin, half mad with fury.

'All right,' said Noah, scratching his head, 'that's just what it was.'

'What did they say about last Sunday?'

'About last Sunday!' replied Noah, considering. 'Why, I told yer that before.'

'Again! Tell it again,' cried Fagin, tightening his grasp on Sikes, and brandishing his other hand aloft, as the foam flew from his lips.

'They asked her,' said Noah, who as he grew more wakeful, seemed to have a dawning perception who Sikes was, 'they asked her why she didn't come last Sunday as she promised. She said she couldn't.'

'Why—why? Tell him that.'

'Because she was forcibly kept at home by Bill, the man she'd told them of before,' replied Noah.

'What more of him?' cried Fagin. 'What more of the man she had told them of before? Tell him that, tell him that.'

'Why, that she couldn't very easily get out of doors unless he knew where she was going to,' said Noah; 'so the first time she went to see the lady, she—ha! ha! ha! it made me laugh when she said it—that it did—she gave him a drink of laudanum.'

'Hell's fire,' cried Sikes, breaking fiercely from the Jew. 'Let me go!'

Flinging the old man from him he rushed from the room and darted, wildly and furiously, up the stairs.

'Bill, Bill!' cried Fagin, following him hastily. 'A word! Only a word. You won't be—too—violent, Bill?'

The day was breaking and there was light enough for the men to see each other's faces. They exchanged one brief glance; there was fire in the eyes of both, which could not be mistaken.

Sikes made no reply but pulling open the door, of which Fagin had turned the lock, dashed into the silent streets.

Without one pause or moment's consideration, the robber held on his headlong course until he reached his own door. He opened it softly with a key, strode lightly up the stairs, and entering his own room, double-locked the door, and lifting a heavy table against it, drew back the curtain of the bed.

The girl was lying half-dressed upon it. He had roused her from her sleep, for she raised herself with a hurried and startled look.

'Get up!' said the man.

'It is you, Bill,' said the girl, with an expression of pleasure at his return.

'It is,' was the reply, 'get up.'

'Bill,' said the girl, in a low voice of alarm, 'why do you look like that at me?'

The robber sat regarding her for a few seconds with dilated nostrils and heaving breast, and then, grasping her by the head and throat, dragged her into the middle of the room, and looking once towards the door, placed his heavy hand upon her mouth.

'Bill, Bill!' gasped the girl, wrestling with the strength of mortal fear—'I won't scream or cry—not once—hear me—speak to me—tell me what I have done!'

'You know, you she-devil!' returned the robber, suppressing his breath. 'You were watched tonight; every word you said was heard.'

'Then spare my life, for the love of heaven, as I spared yours,' rejoined the girl, clinging to him.

The man struggled violently to release his arms; but those of the girl were clasped round his, and tear her as he would, he could not tear them away.

The housebreaker freed one arm and grasped his pistol. The certainty of immediate detection if he fired flashed across his mind even in the midst of his fury, and he beat it twice with all the force he could summon, upon the upturned face that almost touched his own.

She staggered and fell, blinded with the blood that rained down from a deep cut in her forehead, but, raising herself with difficulty on her knees, drew from her bosom a white handkerchief—Rose Maylie's own—and holding it up in her folded hands, as high towards heaven as her feeble strength would allow, breathed one prayer for mercy to her Maker.

It was a ghastly figure to look upon. The murderer, staggering backward to the wall and shutting out the sight with his hand, seized a heavy club and struck her down.

* * * *

Of all the horrors that rose with an ill scent upon the morning air, that was the foulest and most cruel. The sun, bursting upon the crowded city in clear and radiant glory, lighted up the room where the murdered woman lay. If the sight had been a ghastly one in the dull morning, what was it now, in all that brilliant light!

Sikes had not moved. He had been afraid to stir. There was the body—mere flesh and blood, no more—but such flesh, and so much blood!

He struck a light, kindled a fire, and thrust the club into it to burn away and smoulder to ashes. He washed himself, and rubbed his clothes; where the spots would not be removed he cut the pieces out and burnt them. He then shut the door softly, locked it, took the key and left the house. He whistled on the dog and walked rapidly away.

He went through Islington, strode up the hill at Highgate on which stands the stone in honour of Whittington, turned down to Highgate Hill, unsteady of purpose and uncertain where to go. Finally he came out at Hampstead Heath and in one of the fields at North End, laid himself under a hedge and slept.

Soon he was up again and away—not far into the country—but back towards London by the high road—then back again. He walked till he almost dropped upon the ground, then lay down in a lane and had a long but broken and uneasy sleep. He wandered on again, irresolute and undecided, and oppressed with the fear of another solitary night.

Suddenly he took the desperate resolution of going back to London. 'There's somebody there to speak to, at all events. They'll never expect to nab me there. Why can't I lie by for a week or so, and forcing blunt from Fagin, get abroad to France?'

He acted upon this impulse without delay, resolved to lie concealed within a short distance of the metropolis and enter it at dusk by a circuitous route.

The dog, though—if any descriptions of him were out, this might lead to his apprehension as he passed along the streets. Resolved to drown him, he halted at the brink of a pool and called him.

Perhaps the dog's instinct apprehended something of his master's purpose. The animal advanced, retreated, paused an instant, turned and scoured away at his hardest speed.

12

JUSTICE WINS AT LAST

THE twilight was beginning to close in when Mr. Brownlow alighted from a hackney-coach at his own door and knocked softly. The door being opened, a sturdy man got out of the coach and stationed himself on one side of the steps, while another man who had been seated on the box, dismounted too and stood upon the other side. At a sign from Mr. Brownlow they helped out a third man, and taking him between them, hurried into the house. This man was Monks.

They walked in the same manner up the stairs without speaking, and Mr. Brownlow, preceding them, led the way into a back room. At the door of this apartment, Monks, who had ascended with evident reluctance, stopped, but reading in the old gentleman's countenance nothing but severity and determination, walked into the room and, shrugging his shoulders, sat down.

'Lock the door on the outside,' said Mr. Brownlow to the attendants, 'and come when I ring.'

The men obeyed and the two were left alone together.

'This is pretty treatment, sir,' said Monks, throwing down his hat and cloak, 'from my father's oldest friend.'

'It is because I was your father's oldest friend, young man,' returned Mr. Brownlow; 'it is because the hopes and wishes of young and happy years were bound up with him and that fair creature of his blood and kindred who rejoined her God in youth and left me here a solitary and lonely man: it is because he knelt with me beside his only sister's death-bed when he was yet a boy on the morning that would—but Heaven willed otherwise—have made her my young wife; it is because my seared heart clung to him from that time forth, through all his trials and errors till he died; it is because old recollections and associations filled my heart, and even the sight of you brings with it old thoughts of him; it is because

of all these things that I am moved to treat you gently now—
yes, Edward Leeford—even now—and blush for your
unworthiness who bear the name.'

'What has the name to do with it?' asked the other, after
contemplating, half in silence and half in dogged wonder, the
agitation of his companion. 'What is the name to me?'

'Nothing,' replied Mr. Brownlow, 'nothing to you. But it
was hers, and even at this distance of time brings back to me,
an old man, the glow and thrill which I once felt, only to hear
it repeated by a stranger. I am very glad you have changed
it—very—very.'

'This is all mighty fine,' said Monks. 'But what do you
want with me?'

'You have a brother,' said Mr. Brownlow, rousing himself,
'a brother, the whisper of whose name in your ear when I
came behind you in the street was in itself almost enough to
make you accompany me hither, in wonder and alarm.'

'I have no brother,' replied Monks. 'You know I was an
only child. Why do you talk to me of my brother? You know
that as well as I.'

'Attend to what I do know, and you may not,' said Mr.
Brownlow. 'I shall interest you by and by. I know that of the
wretched marriage into which family pride, and the most
sordid and narrowest of all ambition, forced your unhappy
father when a mere boy, you were the sole and most unnatural
issue.'

'I don't care for hard names,' interrupted Monks with a
leering laugh. 'You know the fact and that's enough for me.'

'But I also know,' pursued the old gentleman, 'the misery,
the slow torture, the protracted anguish of that ill-assorted
union, until at last, they wrenched the clanking bond asunder
and, retiring a wide space apart, carried each a galling fragment
of which nothing but death could break the rivets, to hide
it in new society beneath the gayest looks they could assume.
Your mother succeeded; she forgot it soon. But it rusted and
cankered at your father's heart for years.

'Well, they were separated,' said Monks, 'and what of that?'

'When they had been separated for some time,' resumed Mr.
Brownlow, 'and your mother, wholly given up to continental
frivolities, had utterly forgotten the young husband ten good

years her junior, who, with prospects blighted, lingered on at home, he fell among new friends. *This* circumstance, at least, you know already.'

'Not I,' said Monks, turning away his eyes and beating his foot upon the ground, as a man who is determined to deny everything. 'Not I.'

'Your manner, no less than your actions, assures me that you have never forgotten it, or ceased to think of it with bitterness,' returned Mr. Brownlow. 'I speak of fifteen years ago, when you were not more than eleven years old, and your father but one-and-thirty—for he was, I repeat, a boy, when his father ordered him to marry. Must I go back to events which cast a shade upon the memory of your parent, or will you spare it and disclose to me the truth?'

'I have nothing to disclose,' rejoined Monks. 'You must talk on if you will.'

'These new friends, then,' said Mr. Brownlow, 'were a Naval officer retired from active service whose wife had died but half a year before and left him with two children—there had been more, but of all their family happily but two survived. They were both daughters, one a beautiful creature of nineteen and the other a mere child of two or three years old.'

'What's this to me?' asked Monks.

'They resided,' said Mr. Brownlow, without seeming to hear the interruption, 'in a part of the country to which your father, in his wandering, had repaired, and where he had taken up his abode. As the old officer knew him more and more, he grew to love him. I would that it had ended there. His daughter did the same.'

The old man paused; Monks was biting his lips, with his eyes fixed on the floor; seeing this, he immediately resumed:

'The end of a year found him contracted, solemnly contracted to that daughter, the object of the first, true, ardent, only passion of a guileless girl. At length one of those rich relations to strengthen whose interest and importance your father had been sacrificed—died, and to repair the misery he had been instrumental in occasioning, left him *his* panacea for all griefs—money. It was necessary that he should immediately repair to Rome, whither this man had sped for health and where he had died, leaving his affairs in great confusion. He went, was seized with mortal illness there; was followed, the moment the intelligence reached Paris, by your mother, who carried you with her; he died the day after her arrival, leaving no will—*no will*—so that the whole property fell to her and you. Before he went abroad, and as he passed through London on his way,' said Mr. Brownlow slowly, and fixing his eyes upon the other's face, 'he came to me.'

'I never heard of that,' interrupted Monks in a tone intended to appear incredulous, but savouring more of disagreeable surprise.

'He came to me, and left with me, among some other things, a picture—a portrait painted by himself—a likeness of this poor girl—which he did not wish to leave behind, and could not carry forward on his hasty journey. He was torn by anxiety and remorse almost to a shadow; talked in a wild and distracted way of ruin and dishonour worked by himself; confided to me his intention to convert his whole property, at any loss, into money and, having settled on his wife and you a portion of his recent acquisition, to fly the country—I guessed too well he would not fly alone—and never see it more. Even from me, his old and early friend, whose strong attachment had taken root in the earth that covered one most dear to both—even from me he withheld any more particular confession, promising to write and tell me all, and after that to see me once again, for the last time on earth. Alas! *That* was the last time. I had no letter, and I never saw him more.

'I went,' said Mr. Brownlow, after a short pause, 'I went, when all was over, to the scene of his—I will use the term the world would freely use, for worldly harshness or favour are now alike to him—of his guilty love, resolved that if my fears were realised that erring child should find one heart and home to shelter and compassionate her. The family had left that part a week before; they had called in such trifling debts as were outstanding, discharged them and left the place by night. Why, or whither, none can tell.'

Monks drew his breath more freely, and looked round with a smile of triumph.

'When your brother,' said Mr. Brownlow, drawing nearer to the other's chair, 'when your brother—a feeble, ragged, neglected child—was cast in my way by a stronger hand than chance, and rescued by me from a life of vice and infamy——'

'What?' cried Monks.

'By me,' said Mr. Brownlow. 'I told you I should interest you before long. I say by me—I see that your cunning associate suppressed my name, although for aught he knew, it would be quite strange to your ears. When he was rescued by me, then, and lay recovering from sickness in my house, his strong resemblance to this picture I have spoken of, struck me with astonishment. Even when I first saw him in all his dirt and misery, there was a lingering expression in his face that came upon me like a glimpse of some old friend flashing on one in a vivid dream. I need not tell you he was snared away before I knew his history——'

'Why not?' asked Monks hastily.

'Because you know it well.'

'I!'

'Denial to me is vain,' replied Mr. Brownlow. 'I shall show you that I know more than that.'

'You—you can't prove anything against me,' stammered Monks, 'I defy you to do it!'

'We shall see,' returned the old gentleman with a searching glance. 'I lost the boy and no efforts of mine could recover him. Your mother being dead, I knew that you alone could solve the mystery if anybody could, and as when I had last heard of you you were on your own estate on the West Indies—whither, as you well know, you retired on your mother's death to escape the consequences of vicious courses here—I made the voyage. You had left it months before and were supposed to be in London, but no-one could tell where. I returned. Your agents had no clue to your residence. You came and went, they said, as strangely as you had ever done—sometimes for days together, and sometimes for months—keeping to all appearance the same low haunts and mingling with the same infamous herd who had been your associates when you were a fierce, ungovernable boy. I wearied them with new applications. I paced the streets by night and day; but until two hours ago all my efforts were fruitless, and I never saw you for an instant.'

'And now you do see me,' said Monks, rising boldly, 'what

then? Fraud and robbery are high-sounding words—justified you think by a fancied resemblance in some young imp to an idle daub of a dead man's brother! You don't even know that a child was born of this maudlin pair; you don't even know that.'

'I *did not*,' replied Mr. Brownlow, rising too, 'but within the last fortnight I have learnt it all. You have a brother; you know it and him. There was a will which your mother destroyed, leaving the secret and the gain to you at her own death. It contained a reference to some child likely to be the result of this sad connection, which child was born and accidentally encountered by you, when your suspicions were first awakened by his resemblance to his father. You repaired to the place of his birth. There existed proofs—proofs long suppressed—of his birth and parentage. Those proofs were destroyed by you, and now, in your own words to your accomplice the Jew, "the only proofs of the boy's identity lie at the bottom of the river, and the old hag that received them from the mother is rotting in her coffin". Unworthy son, coward, liar—you, Edward Leeford, do you still brave me?'

'No, no, no!' returned the coward, overwhelmed by these accumulated charges.

'Every word,' cried the old gentleman, 'every word that has passed between you and this detested villain, is known to me. Murder has been done to which you are morally if not really a party.'

'No, no,' interposed Monks. 'I—I—know nothing of that; I was going to inquire the truth of the story when you overtook me. I didn't know the cause; I thought it was a common quarrel.'

'It was the partial disclosure of your secrets,' replied Mr. Brownlow. 'Will you disclose the whole?'

'Yes, I will.'

'Set your hand to a statement of truth and facts, and repeat it before witnesses?'

'That I promise too.'

'Remain quietly here until such a document is drawn up, and proceed with me to such a place as I may deem most advisable, for the purpose of attesting it?'

'If you insist on that, I'll do that also,' replied Monks.

'You must do more than that,' said Mr. Brownlow. 'Make restitution to an innocent and unoffending child, for such he is, although the offspring of a guilty and most miserable love. You have not forgotten the provisions of the will. Carry them into execution so far as your brother is concerned, and then go where you please. In this world you and I need meet no more.'

While Monks was pacing up and down, meditating with dark and evil looks on this proposal and the possibilities of evading it, torn by his fears on the one hand and his hatred on the other, the door was hurriedly unlocked, and a gentleman (Mr. Losberne) entered the room in violent agitation.

'The man will be taken!' he cried. 'He will be taken tonight!'

'The murderer?' asked Mr. Brownlow.

'Yes, yes,' replied the other. 'His dog has been seen lurking about some old haunt, and there seems little doubt that his master is or will be there, under cover of the darkness. Spies are hovering about in every direction. I have spoken with the men who are charged with his capture, and they tell me he cannot escape. A reward of a hundred pounds is proclaimed by Government tonight.'

'I will give fifty more,' said Mr. Brownlow, 'and proclaim it with my own lips upon the spot, if I can reach it. Where is Mr. Maylie?'

'Harry? As soon as he had seen your friend here safe in a coach with you, he hurried off to where he heard this,' replied the doctor, 'and mounting his horse sallied forth to join the first party at some place in the outskirts agreed upon between them.'

'Fagin,' said Mr. Brownlow, 'what of him?'

'When I last heard he had not been taken; but he will be, or is by this time. They're sure of him.'

'Have you made up your mind?' asked Mr. Brownlow, in a low voice, of Monks.

'Yes,' he replied. 'You—you will be secret with me?'

'I will. Remain here until I return. It is your only hope of safety.'

They left the room and the door was again locked.

'What have you done?' asked the doctor in a whisper.

'All I could hope to do, and even more. But my blood boils to avenge this poor murdered creature. Which way have they taken?'

'Drive straight to the office and you will be in time.' replied Mr. Losberne, 'and I will remain here.'

The two gentlemen hastily separated, each in a fever of excitement wholly uncontrollable.

Near to that part of the Thames on which the church at Rotherhithe abuts, where the buildings on the banks are dirtiest and the vessels on the river are blackest with the dust of colliers and the smoke of close-built low-roofed houses, there exists the filthiest, the strangest, the most extraordinary of the many localities that are hidden in London, wholly unknown, even by name, to the great mass of its inhabitants.

In such a neighbourhood, beyond Dockhead, in the Borough of Southwark, stands Jacob's Island, surrounded by a muddy ditch six or eight feet deep, and eighteen or twenty wide when the tide is in, once called Mill Pond but known in the days of this story as Folly Ditch. It is a creek or inlet from the Thames and can always be filled at highwater by opening the sluices at the Lead Mills from which it took its old name.

In Jacob's Island the warehouses are roofless and empty, the walls are crumbling down, the windows are no more, the doors are falling into the streets, the chimneys are blackened but they yield no smoke. Thirty or forty years ago, before losses and chancery suits came upon it, it was a thriving place. They must have powerful motives for a secret residence or be reduced to a destitute condition indeed, who seek a refuge in Jacob's Island.

In an upper room in one of these houses—a detached house of fair size, ruinous in other respects, but strongly defended at door and window, of which house the back commanded the ditch in such a manner already described—there were assembled three men who, regarding each other every now and then with looks expressing perplexity and expectation, sat for some time in profound and gloomy silence. One of these was Toby Crackit, another Mr. Chitling, and the third a robber of fifty years whose nose had been almost beaten in, a returned transport and his name was Kags.

'I wish,' said Toby, turning to Mr. Chitling, 'that you and I picked out some other crib when the two old ones got too warm, and had not come here, my fine feller.'

'Why didn't you, blunder-head!' said Kags.

'Well, I thought you'd have been a little more glad to see me than this,' replied Mr. Chitling with a melancholy air.

There was a short silence, after which Toby Crackit, seeming to abandon as hopeless any further effort to maintain his usual devil-may-care swagger, turned to Chitling and said:

'When was Fagin took, then?'

'Just at dinner-time—two o'clock this afternoon. Charlotte and I made our lucky up the wash'us chimney, and Noah got into the empty water-butt, head downwards; but his legs were so precious long that they stuck out at the top, and so they took him too.'

'And Bet?'

'Poor Bet! She went to see the Body, to speak to who it was,' replied Chitling, his countenance falling more and more, 'and went off mad, screaming and raving and beating her head against the boards; so they put a strait-weskit on her and took her to the hospital—and there she is.'

'Wot's become of young Bates?' demanded Kags.

'He hung about, not to come over here afore dark, but he'll be here soon,' replied Chitling. 'There's nowhere else to go now, for the people at the Cripples are all in custody, and the bar of the ken—I went up there and see it with my own eyes— is filled with traps.'

'This is a smash,' observed Toby, biting his lips. 'There's more than one will go with this.'

'The sessions are on,' said Kags. 'If they get the inquest over and Noah turns King's evidence—as of course he will from what he's said already—they can prove Fagin an accessor before the fact and get the trial on on Friday, and he'll swing in six days from this, by G . . . !'

While the men sat in silence with their eyes fixed upon the floor, a pattering noise was heard upon the stairs and Sikes's dog bounded into the room. They ran to the window, downstairs and into the street. The dog had jumped in at an open window; he made no attempt to follow them, nor was his master to be seen.

'What's the meaning of this?' said Toby, when they had returned. 'He can't be coming here. I—I—hope not.'

'If he was coming here, he'd have come with the dog,' said Kags, stooping down to examine the animal, who lay panting on the floor. 'Here! Give us some water for him; he has run himself faint.'

'He's drunk it all up, every drop,' said Chitling after watching the dog some time in silence. 'Covered with mud—lame—half-blind—he must have come a long way.'

'No' said Kags, 'I think Sikes has got out of the country, and left the dog behind. He must have given him the slip somehow, or he wouldn't be so easy.'

This solution, appearing the most probable one, was adopted as the right; the dog, creeping under a chair, coiled himself up to sleep, without more notice from anybody.

The men had sat for some time when suddenly was heard a hurried knocking at the door below.

Crackit went to the window, and shaking all over, drew in his head. There was no need to tell them who it was; his pale face was enough. The dog too, was on the alert in an instant and ran whining to the door.

Crackit went down to the door and returned followed by a man with the lower part of his face buried in a handkerchief and another tied over his head under his hat. He drew them slowly off. Blanched face, sunken eyes, hollow cheeks, beard of three day's growth, wasted flesh, short thick breath: it was the very ghost of Sikes.

'How came that dog here?' he asked.

'Alone. Three hours ago.'

'Tonight's paper says that Fagin's took. Is it true or a lie?'

'True?'

They were silent again.

'You that keep this house,' said Sikes, turning his face to Crackit, 'do you mean to sell me or to let me lie here till this hunt is over?'

'You may stop here if you think it's safe,' returned the person addressed, after some hesitation.

Sikes carried his eyes slowly up the wall behind him, rather trying to turn his head than actually doing it, and said:

'Is—it—the body—is it buried?'

They shook their heads.

'Who's that knocking?'

Crackit intimated by a motion of his hand as he left the room, that there was nothing to fear, and directly came back with Charley Bates behind him. Sikes sat opposite the door, so that the moment the boy entered the room he encountered his figure.

'Toby,' said the boy, falling back, as Sikes turned his eyes towards him, 'why didn't you tell me this downstairs? Let me go into some other room,' said the boy, retreating still farther.

'Charley!' said Sikes, stepping forward. 'Don't you—don't you know me?'

'Don't come nearer me,' answered the boy, still retreating, and looking with horror in his eyes upon the murderer's face. 'You monster!'

The boy actually flung himself single-handed upon the strong man, and in the intensity of his energy and the suddenness or his surprise, brought him heavily to the ground.

The three spectators seemed quite stupefied. They offered no interference, and the boy and man rolled on the ground together—the former heedless of the blows that showered upon him, wrenching his hands tighter and tighter in the garments about the murderer's breast, and never ceasing to call for help with all his might.

The contest, however, was too unequal to last long. Sikes had the boy down and his knee was on his throat, when Crackit pulled him back with a look of alarm and pointed to the window. There were lights gleaming below, voices in loud and earnest conversation, the tramp of hurried footsteps —endless they seemed in number—crossing the nearest wooden bridge. There came a loud knocking at the door, and then a hoarse murmur from such a multitude of angry voices as would have made the boldest quail.

'Help!' shrieked the boy in a voice that rent the air. 'He's here! Break down the door!'

'In the King's name!' cried the voices without; and the hoarse cry rose again, but louder.

'Break down the door!' screamed the boy. 'I tell you they'll never open it. Run straight to the room where the light is. Break down the door!'

'Open the door of some place where I can lock this screeching Hell-babe,' cried Sikes fiercely, dragging the boy, now, as easily as if he were an empty sack. 'That door—quick!' He flung him in, bolted it, and turned the key.

Strokes, thick and heavy, rattled upon the chained door downstairs and lower window-shutters, and a loud hurrah burst from the crowd.

'Damn you!' cried the desperate ruffian, throwing up the sash and menacing the crowd. 'Do your worst! I'll cheat you yet!'

Of all the terrific yells that ever fell on mortal ears, none could exceed the cry of the infuriated throng. Some shouted to those who were nearest to set the house on fire; others roared to the officers to shoot him dead. Among them all none showed such fury as the man on horseback, who, throwing himself out of the saddle and bursting through the crowd as if he were parting water, cried beneath the window in a voice that rose above all others, 'Twenty guineas to the man who brings a ladder!'

'The tide,' cried the murderer, as he staggered back into the room and shut the faces out, 'the tide was in as I came up. Give me a rope, a long rope. They're all in front. I may drop into the Folly Ditch and clear off that way. Give me a rope, or I shall do three more murders and kill myself.'

The panic-stricken men pointed to where such articles were kept; the murderer, hastily selecting the longest and strongest cord, hurried up to the house-top.

All the windows in the rear of the house had been long ago bricked up, except one small trap in the room where the boy was locked, and that was too small even for the passage of his body. But from this aperture he had never ceased to call on those without, to guard the back; and thus, when the murderer emerged at last on the house-top by the door in the roof, a loud shout proclaimed the fact to those in front, who immediately began to pour round, pressing upon each other in an unbroken stream.

He planted a board, which he had carried up with him for the purpose, so firmly against the door that it must be a matter of great difficulty to open it from the inside, and creeping over the tiles looked over the low parapet.

The water was out and the ditch a bed of mud.

'They have him now!' cried a man on the nearest bridge. 'Hurrah!'

The crowd grew light with uncovered heads, and again the shout arose.

'I will give fifty pounds,' cried an old gentleman from the same quarter, 'to the man who takes him alive. I will remain here till he comes to ask me for it.'

There was another roar. At this moment the word was passed among the crowd that the door was forced at last, and that he who had first called for the ladder had mounted into the room. The stream abruptly turned as this intelligence ran from mouth to mouth; and the people at the windows, seeing those upon the bridges pouring back, quitted their stations and, running into the street, joined the concourse that now thronged pell-mell to the spot they had left, each man crushing and striving with his neighbour and all panting with impatience to get near the door and look upon the criminal as the officers brought him out.

The man sprang upon his feet determined to make one last effort for his life by dropping into the ditch, and at the risk of being stifled, endeavouring to creep away in the darkness and confusion. Roused into new strength and energy, and stimulated by the noise within the house which announced that an entrance had really been affected, he set his foot against the stack of chimneys, fastened one end of the rope tightly and firmly around it, and with the other made a strong running noose with the aid of his hands and teeth almost in a second. He could let himself down by the cord to within a less distance of the ground than his own height, and had his knife ready in his hand to cut it then and drop.

At the very instant that he brought the loop over his head previous to slipping it beneath his arm-pits, and when the old gentleman before-mentioned (who had clung so tight to the railing of the bridge as to resist the force of the crowd and retain his position) earnestly warned those about him that the man was about to lower himself down—at that very instant the murderer, looking behind him on the roof, threw his arms above his head and uttered a yell of terror.

'The eyes again!' he cried in an unearthly screech.

Staggering as if struck by lightning, he lost his balance and tumbled over the parapet. The noose was on his neck. It ran up with his weight, tight as a bow string and swift as the arrow it speeds. He fell for five-and-thirty feet. There was a sudden jerk, a terrific convulsion of the limbs; and there he hung with the open knife clenched in his stiffening hand.

The old chimney quivered with the shock but stood it bravely. The murderer swung lifeless against the wall; and the boy, thrusting aside the dangling body which obscured his view, called to the people to come and take him out, for God's sake.

A dog, which had lain concealed till now, ran backwards and forwards on the parapet with a dismal howl, and collecting himself for a spring jumped for the dead man's shoulders. Missing his aim he fell into the ditch, turning completely over as he went, and striking his head against a stone, dashed out his brains.

* * * *

These events were yet but two days old when Oliver found himself, at three o'clock in the afternoon, in a travelling carriage rolling fast towards his native town. Mrs. Maylie and Rose, and Mrs. Bedwin, and the good doctor were with him; and Mr. Brownlow followed in a post-chaise, accompanied by one other person whose name had not been mentioned.

Oliver and the two ladies had carefully been made acquainted by Mr. Brownlow of the nature of the admissions which had been forced from Monks; and although they knew the object of their present journey was to complete the work that had been so well begun, still the whole matter was enveloped in enough of doubt and mystery to leave them in endurance of the most intense suspense.

The same kind friend had, with Mr. Losberne's assistance, cautiously stopped all channels of communication through which they could receive intelligence of the dreadful occurrences that had so recently taken place.

But if Oliver, under these influences, had remained silent while they journeyed towards his birthplace by a road he had

never seen, how the whole current of his recollections ran
back to old times, and what a crowd of emotions were
wakened up in his breast when they turned into that which he
had traversed on foot—a poor, houseless wandering boy,
without a friend to help him or a roof to shelter his head.

'See there, there!' cried Oliver, eagerly clasping the hand
of Rose, and pointing out at the carriage window; 'that's the
stile I came over; those are the hedges I crept behind for
fear anyone should overtake me and force me back! Yonder is
the path across the fields, leading to the old house where I was
a little child! Oh Dick, Dick, my dear old friend, if I could
only see you now!'

As they approached the town and drove through its narrow
streets, it became matter of no small difficulty to restrain the
boy within reasonable bounds. There was Sowerberry's the
undertaker's just as it used to be, only smaller and less imposing in appearance than he remembered it—there were all
the well-known shops and houses, with almost every one of
which he had some slight incident connected—there was
Gamfield's cart, the very cart he used to have, standing at the
public house door—there was the workhouse, the dreary
prison of his youthful days, with its dismal windows frowning
on the street—there was the same lean porter standing at the
gate, at sight of whom Oliver involuntarily shrunk back, and
then laughed at himself for being so foolish, then cried, then
laughed again—there were scores of faces at the doors and
windows that he knew quite well—there was nearly everything
as if he had left it but yesterday and all his recent life had been
but a happy dream.

But it was pure, earnest, joyful reality. They drove straight
to the door of the chief hotel (which Oliver used to stare up
at with awe and think a mighty palace); and there was Mr.
Grimwig all ready to receive them, kissing the young lady and
the old one too, when they got out of the coach, as if he were
the grandfather of the whole party, all smiles and kindness
and not offering to eat his head, no not once. There was
dinner prepared and there were bedrooms ready, and everything was arranged as if by magic.

Notwithstanding all this, when the hurry of the first half-
hour was over, the same silence and constraint prevailed that

had marked their journey down. Mr. Brownlow did not join them at dinner but remained in a separate room. The two other gentlemen hurried in and out with anxious faces, and during the short intervals when they were present, conversed apart. Once Mrs. Maylie was called away and, after being absent for nearly an hour, returned with eyes swollen with weeping. All these things made Rose and Oliver, who were not in any new secrets, nervous and uncomfortable.

At length, when nine o'clock had come and they began to think they were to hear no more that night, Mr. Losberne and Mr. Grimwig entered the room, followed by Mr. Brownlow and a man whom Oliver almost shrieked with surprise to see; for they told him it was his brother, and it was the same man he had met at the market-town and seen looking in with Fagin at the window of his little room. Monks cast a look of hate, which even then, he could not dissemble at the astonished boy, and sat down near the door. Mr. Brownlow, who had papers in his hand, walked to a table near which Rose and Oliver were seated.

'This is a painful task,' said he, 'but these declarations which have been signed in London before many gentlemen, must be in substance repeated here. I would have spared you the degradation but we must hear them from your own lips before we part, and you know why.'

'Go on,' said the person addressed, turning away his face. 'Quick. I have almost done enough, I think. Don't keep me here.'

'This child,' said Mr. Brownlow, drawing Oliver to him, and laying his hand upon his head, 'is your half-brother: the illegitimate son of your father, my dear friend Edwin Leeford, by poor young Agnes Fleming, who died in giving him birth.'

'Yes,' said Monks, scowling at the trembling boy, the beating of whose heart he might have heard. 'That is their bastard child.'

'The term you use,' said Mr. Brownlow sternly, 'is a reproach to those long since passed beyond the feeble censure of the world. It reflects disgrace on no one living except you who use it. Let that pass. He was born in this town.'

'In the workhouse of this town,' was the sullen reply. 'You

have the story there.' He pointed impatiently to the papers as he spoke.

'I must have it here too,' said Mr. Brownlow, looking round upon the listeners.

'Listen then! You!' returned Monks. 'His father being taken ill at Rome was joined by his wife, my mother, from whom he had long been separated, who went from Paris and took me with her—to look after his property for what I know, for she had no great affection for him, nor he for her. He knew nothing of us, for his senses were gone and he slumbered on till next day, when he died. Among the papers in his desk were two, dated on the night his illness first came on, directed to yourself—' he addressed himself to Mr. Brownlow—'and enclosed in a few short lines to you, with an intimation on the cover of the package that it was not to be forwarded until after he was dead, One of these papers was a letter to this girl, Agnes, the other a will.'

'What of the letter?' asked Mr. Brownlow.

'The letter? A sheet of paper crossed and crossed again, with a penitent confession and prayers to God to help her. He had palmed a tale on the girl that some secret mystery—to be explained one day—prevented his marrying her just then; and so she had gone on, trusting patiently to him, until she trusted too far and lost what none could give her back. She was, at that time, within a few months of her confinement. He told her all he had meant to do to hide her shame if he had lived, and prayed her, if he died, not to curse his memory or think the consequences of their sin would be visited on her or their young child; for all the guilt was his. He reminded her of the day he had given her a little locket and ring with her Christian name engraved on it and a blank left for that which he hoped one day to have bestowed upon her—prayed her yet to keep it and wear it next her heart, as he had done before—and then ran on wildly, in the same words, over and over again, as if he had gone distracted. I believe he had.'

'The will,' said Mr. Brownlow, as Oliver's tears fell fast. Monks was silent.

'The will,' said Mr. Brownlow, speaking for him, 'was in the same spirit as the letter. He talked of miseries which his wife had brought upon him; of the rebellious disposition, vice, malice, and premature bad passions of you, his only son, who had been trained to hate him; and left you and your mother each an annuity of eight hundred pounds. The bulk of his property he divided into two equal portions—one for Agnes Fleming and the other for their child, if it should be born alive and ever come of age. If it were a girl, it was to inherit the money unconditionally, but if a boy, only on the stipulation that in his minority he should never have stained his name with any public act of dishonour, meanness, cowardice or wrong. He did this, he said, to mark his confidence in the mother and his conviction—only strengthened by approaching death—that the child would share her gentle heart and noble nature. If he were disappointed in this expectation, then the money was to come to you; for then, and not till then, when both children were equal, would he recognise your prior claim upon his purse, who had none upon his heart and had, from an infant, repulsed him with coldness and aversion.'

'My mother,' said Monks, in a louder tone, 'did what a woman should have done. She burnt this will. The letter never reached its destination; but that and other proofs she kept in case they ever tried to lie away the blot. The girl's father had the truth from her with every aggravation that her violent hate—I love her for it now—could add. Goaded by shame and dishonour he fled with his children into a remote corner of Wales, changing his very name, that his friends might never know of his retreat; and here, no great while afterwards, he was found dead in his bed. The girl had left her home, in secret, some weeks before; he had searched for her on foot in every town and village near; it was on the night when he returned home, assured that she had destroyed herself to hide her shame, that his old heart broke.'

There was a short silence here, until Mr. Brownlow took up the thread of the narrative.

'Years after this,' he said, 'this man's—Edward Leeford's —mother came to me. He had left her when only eighteen; robbed her of jewels and money; gambled, squandered, forged and fled to London, where for two years he had associated with the lowest outcasts. She was sinking under a painful and incurable disease and wished to recover him before she died.

Inquiries were set on foot and strict searches made. They were unavailing for a long time, but ultimately successful, and he went back with her to France.'

'There she died,' said Monks, 'after a lingering illness; and on her deathbed she bequeathed these secrets to me, together with her unquenchable and deadly hatred of all whom they involved—though she need not have left me that, for I had inherited it long before. She would not believe that the girl had destroyed herself, and the child too, but was filled with the impression that a male child had been born and was alive. I swore to her, if ever it crossed my path, to hunt it down, never to let it rest, to pursue it with the bitterest and most unrelenting animosity, to vent upon it the hatred that I deeply felt, and to spit upon the empty vaunt of that insulting will by dragging it, if I could, to the very gallows-foot. She was right. He came in my way at last. I began well; and but for babbling drabs, I would have finished as I began!'

As the villain folded his arms tight together and muttered curses to the terrified group beside him and explained that the Jew, who had been his old accomplice and confidant, had a large reward for keeping Oliver ensnared, of which some part was to be given up in the event of his being rescued, and that a dispute on this head had led to their visit to the country house for the purpose of identifying him.

'The locket and ring?' said Mr. Brownlow, turning to Monks.

'I bought them from the man and woman I told you of, who stole them from the nurse, who stole them from the corpse,' answered Monks, without raising his eyes.

Mr. Brownlow merely nodded to Mr. Grimwig, who, disappearing with great alacrity, shortly returned, pushing in Mrs. Bumble and dragging her unwilling consort after him.

'Do my heyes deceive me!' cried Mr. Bumble, with ill-feigned enthusiasm, 'or is that little Oliver? Oh, O-li-ver, if you knowed how I've been a-grieving for you——'

'Hold your tongue, fool,' murmured Mrs. Bumble.

'Come, sir,' said Mr. Grimwig, tartly; 'suppress you feelings.'

Mr. Brownlow had stepped up to within a short distance of the respectable couple. He inquired, as he pointed to Monks:

'Do you know that person?'

'No,' replied Mrs. Bumble flatly.

'Perhaps you don't?' said Mr. Brownlow, addressing her spouse.

'I never saw him in all my life,' said Mr. Bumble.

'Nor sold him anything, perhaps?'

'No,' replied Mrs. Bumble.

'You never had, perhaps, a certain gold locket and ring?' said Mr. Brownlow.

'Certainly not,' replied the matron. 'Why are we brought here to answer to such nonsense as this?'

Again Mr. Brownlow nodded to Mr. Grimwig; and again that gentleman limped away with extraordinary readiness; this time he led in two palsied women, who shook and tottered as they walked.

'You shut the door the night old Sally died,' said the foremost one, raising her shrivelled hand, 'but you couldn't shut out the sound, nor stop the chinks.'

'No, no,' said the other, looking round her and wagging her toothless jaws, 'no, no, no!'

'We heard her try to tell you what she'd done, and saw you take a paper from her hand, and watched you, too, next day, to the pawnbroker's shop,' said the first.

'Yes,' said the second, 'it was a locket and gold ring. We found out that and saw it given you. We were by. Oh, we were by.'

'And we know more than that,' resumed the first, 'for she often told us, long ago, that the young mother had told her that, feeling she should never get over it, she was on her way at the time she was taken ill, to die near the grave of the father of the child.'

'Would you like to see the pawnbroker himself?' asked Mr. Grimwig of Mrs. Bumble with a motion towards the door.

'No,' replied the woman, 'if he'—she pointed to Monks—'has been coward enough to confess, as I see he has, and you have sounded all these hags till you have found the right ones, I have nothing more to say. I *did* sell them, and they're where you'll never get them. What then?'

'Nothing,' replied Mr. Brownlow, 'except that it remains for us to take care that neither of you is employed in a situation of trust again. You may leave the room.

'I hope,' said Mr. Bumble, looking about him with great ruefulness, as Mr. Grimwig disappeared with the two old women: 'I hope that this unfortunate little circumstance will not deprive me of my porochial office?'

'Indeed it will,' replied Mr. Brownlow. 'You may make up your mind to that and think yourself well off besides.'

'It was all Mrs. Bumble. She *would* do it,' urged Mr. Bumble, first looking round to ascertain that his partner had left the room.

'That is no excuse,' replied Mr. Brownlow. 'You were present on the occasion of the destruction of these two trinkets and, indeed, are the more guilty of the two, in the eye of the law; for the law supposes that your wife acts under your direction.'

'If the law supposes that,' said Mr. Bumble, squeezing his hat emphatically in his hands, 'the law is a ass—a idiot. If that's the eye of the law, the law's a bachelor; and the worst I wish the law is, that his eye may be opened by experience—by experience.'

Laying great stress on the repetition of these two words, Mr. Bumble fixed his hat on very tight, and, putting his hands in his pockets, followed his helpmate downstairs.

'Young lady,' said Mr. Brownlow, turning to Rose, 'give me your hand. Do not tremble. You need fear not to hear the few remaining words we have to say.'

'If they have—I do not know how they can—have any reference to me,' said Rose, 'pray let me hear them at some other time. I have not strength or spirits now.'

'Nay,' returned the old gentleman, drawing her arm through his; 'you have more fortitude than this, I'm sure. Do you know this young lady, sir?'

'Yes,' replied Monks.

'I never saw you before,' said Rose faintly.

'I have seen you often,' returned Monks.

'The father of the unhappy Agnes had *two* daughters,' said Mr. Brownlow. 'What was the fate of the other—the child?'

'The child,' replied Monks, 'when her father died in a strange place, in a strange name, without a letter, book or scrap of paper that yielded the faintest clue by which his friends or relatives could be traced—the child was taken by some wretched cottagers, who reared it as their own.'

'Go on,' said Mr. Brownlow, signing to Mrs. Maylie to approach. 'Go on!'

'You couldn't find the spot to which these people had repaired,' said Monks, 'but where friendship fails, hatred will often find a way. My mother found it—after a year of cunning search—ay, and found the child.'

'She took it, did she?'

'No. The people were poor, and began to sicken—at least the man did—of their fine humanity; so she left it with them, giving them a small present of money which would not last long, and promised more, which she never meant to send. She didn't quite rely, however, on their discontent and poverty for the child's unhappiness, but told the history of the sister's shame, with such alterations as suited her; bade them take good heed of the child, for she came of bad blood; and told them she was illegitimate and sure to go wrong at one time or another. The circumstances countenanced all this; the people believed it; and there the child dragged on an existence miserable enough even to satisfy us, until a widow lady residing, then, at Chester, saw the girl by chance, pitied her, and took her home. There was some cursed spell, I think, against us, for in spite of all our efforts she remained there and was happy. I lost sight of her two or three years ago, and saw no more until a few months back.'

'Do you see her now?'

'Yes, leaning on your arm.'

'But not the less my niece,' cried Mrs. Maylie, folding the fainting girl in her arms, 'not the less my dearest child. I would not lose her now for all the treasures of the world. My sweet companion, my own dear girl!'

'The only friend I ever had,' cried Rose, clinging to her. 'The kindest, best of friends. My heart will burst. I cannot bear all this.'

'You have borne more, and have been, through all, the best and gentlest creature that ever shed happiness on every one she knew,' said Mrs. Maylie, embracing her tenderly. 'Come, come, my love, remember who this is who waits to clasp you in his arms, poor child! See here—look, look, my dear!'

'Not aunt,' cried Oliver, throwing his arms about her neck. 'I'll never call her aunt—sister, my own dear sister, that something has taught my heart to love so dearly from the first! Rose, dear, darling Rose!'

They were a long, long time alone. A soft tap at the door at length announced that someone was without. Oliver opened it, glided away, and gave place to Harry Maylie.

'I know it all,' he said taking a seat beside the lovely girl. 'Dear Rose, I know it all, and once more I have come to you. My hopes, my wishes, prospects, feeling—every thought in life except my love for you—have undergone a change. I offer you, now, no distinction among a bustling crowd, no mingling with a world of malice and distraction, but a home— a heart and home. There are smiling fields and waving trees in England's richest county and by one village church—mine. Rose, my own!—There stands a rustic dwelling which you can make me prouder of than all the hopes I have renounced. This is my rank and station now, and here I lay it down!'

* * * *

'It's a trying thing, waiting supper for lovers,' said Mr. Grimwig, waking up, and pulling his pocket handkerchief from over his head.

Truth to tell, the supper had been waiting a most unreasonable time. Neither Mrs. Maylie, nor Harry, nor Rose (who all came in together) could offer a word in extenuation.

'I had serious thoughts of eating my head tonight,' said Mr. Grimwig, 'for I began to think I should get nothing else. I'll take the liberty, if you'll allow me, of saluting the bride that is to be.'

Mr. Grimwig lost no time in carrying this notice into effect upon the blushing girl; and the example being contagious, was followed by the doctor and Mr. Brownlow. Some people affirm that Harry Maylie had been observed to set it, originally, in a dark room adjoining; but the best authorities consider this downright scandal, he being young and a clergyman.

'Oliver, my child,' said Mrs. Maylie, 'where have you been and why do you look so sad? There are tears stealing down your face at this moment. What is the matter?"

It is a world of disappointment, often to the hopes we most cherish, and hopes that do our nature the greatest honour.

Poor Dick was dead!

* ● * ●

The court was paved, from floor to floor, with human faces. Inquisitive and eager eyes peered from every inch of space. From the rail before the dock, away into the sharpest angle of the smallest corner in the gallows, all looks were fixed upon one man—Fagin. Before him and behind—above, below, on the right and on the left—he seemed surrounded by a firmament all bright with gleaming eyes.

The judge had ceased to speak, the jury had sought permission to retire, and Fagin waited, still in the same strained attitude of close attention that he had exhibited since the trial began.

At length there was a cry of silence and a breathless look from all towards the door. The jury returned and passed him close. He could glean nothing from their faces; they might as well have been of stone. Perfect stillness ensued—not a rustle—not a breath—Guilty!

The building rang with a tremendous shout, and another, and another, and then it echoed loud groans that gathered strength as they swelled out, like angry thunder. It was a peal of joy from the populace outside, greeting the news that he would die on Monday.

The judge assumed the black cap. The address was solemn and impressive, the sentence fearful to hear, but the prisoner stood like a marble figure without the motion of a nerve, until the jailer put his hand upon his arm and beckoned him away.

Night—dark, dismal, silent night. The boom of every bell as the church-clock struck came laden with one deep hollow sound—Death.

The day passed off—it was gone as soon as it came. Saturday night. He had only one more night to live. As he thought of this, the day broke—Sunday.

It was not until the night of this last awful day that a withering sense of his helpless desperate state came in its full intensity upon his blighted soul. He sat there, awake but dreaming. Eight—nine—ten. Those were real hours treading on each others heels. Where would he be when they came round again? Eleven! Another struck before the voice of the previous hour had ceased to vibrate.

As it did so, the turnkey unlocked the door of the cell where the condemned criminal sat motionless on his bed and two visitors—an elderly gentleman and a young boy—followed him in.

'Fagin,' said the jailer.

'That's me!' cried the Jew, falling instantly into the attitude of listening he had assumed upon his trial. 'An old man, my Lord, a very old, old man!'

'Here,' said the turnkey, laying his hand upon his breast to keep him down. 'Here's somebody wants to see you, to ask you some questions, I suppose. Fagin, Fagin, are you a man?'

'I shan't be one long,' he replied, looking up with a face retaining no human expression but rage and terror. 'Strike them all dead! What right have they to butcher me?'

As he spoke, he caught sight of Oliver and Mr. Brownlow. Shrinking to the furthest corner of the seat, he demanded to know what they wanted there.

'Steady,' said the turnkey, still holding him down. 'Now, sir, tell him what you want. Quick, if you please, for he grows worse as the time gets on.'

'You have some papers,' said Mr. Brownlow, advancing, 'which were placed in your hands, for better security, by a man named Monks.'

'It's all a lie together,' replied Fagin. 'I haven't one—not one.'

'For the love of God,' said Mr. Brownlow solemnly, 'do not say that now, upon the very verge of death; but tell me where they are. You know that Sikes is dead, that Monks has confessed, that there is no hope of any further gain. Where are those papers?'

'Oliver,' cried Fagin, beckoning to him. 'Here, here, let me whisper to you.'

'I am not afraid,' said Oliver in a low voice, as he relinquished Mr. Brownlow's hand.

'The papers,' said Fagin, drawing Oliver towards him, 'are

in a canvas bag in a hole a little way up the chimney in the top front room. I want to talk to you.'

'Yes, yes,' returned Oliver, 'let me say a prayer. Do! Let me say one prayer. Say only one, upon your knees, with me, and we will talk till morning.'

'Outside, outside,' replied Fagin, pushing the boy before him towards the door and looking vacantly over his head. 'Say I've gone to sleep; they'll believe *you*. You can get me out, if you take me so. Now then, now then!'

The door of the cell opened and the attendants returned.

'Press on, press on,' cried Fagin. 'Softly, but not so slow. Faster, faster!'

The men laid hands on him and disengaged Oliver from his grasp. He struggled with the power of desperation for an instant, and then sent up cry upon cry that penetrated even those massive walls and rang in their ears until they reached the open yard.

It was some time before they left the prison. Oliver nearly swooned after this frightful scene, and was so weak for an hour or more, he had not the strength to walk.

Day was dawning when they again emerged. A great multitude had already assembled; the windows were filled with people smoking and playing cards to beguile the time; the crowd were pushing, quarrelling, joking. Everything told of life and animation but one dark cluster of objects in the centre of all—the black stage, the cross beam, the rope, and all the hideous apparatus of death.

13

ENVOI

The fortunes of those who have figured in this tale are nearly closed. The little that remains to their historian to relate is told in few and simple words.

Before three months had passed, Rose Fleming and Harry Maylie were married in the village church which was henceforth to be the scene of the young clergyman's labours; on the same day they entered into possession for their new and happy home.

Mrs. Maylie took up her abode with her son and daughter-in-law, to enjoy, during the tranquil remainder of her days, the greatest felicity that age and worth can know—the contemplation of the happiness of those on whom the warmest affections have been unceasingly bestowed.

It appeared on full and careful investigation, that if the wreck of property remaining in the custody of Monks (which had never prospered either in his hands or in those of his mother) were equally divided between himself and Oliver, it would yield, to each, little more than three thousand pounds. By the provisions of his father's will, Oliver would have been entitled to the whole; but Mr. Brownlow, unwilling to deprive the elder son of the opportunity of retrieving his former vices and pursuing an honest career, proposed this mode of distribution, to which his young charge joyfully acceded.

Monks, still bearing that assumed name, retired with his portion to a distant part of the New World, where, having quickly squandered it, he once more fell into his old courses and, after undergoing a long confinement for some fresh act of fraud and knavery, at length sunk under an attack of his old disorder, and died in prison. As far from home, died the chief remaining members of his friend Fagin's gang.

Mr. Brownlow adopted Oliver as his son. Removing with

him and the old housekeeper to within a mile of the parsonage house, where his dear friends resided, he gratified the only remaining wish of Oliver's warm and earnest heart, and thus linked together a little society whose condition approached as nearly to one of perfect happiness as can ever be known in this changing world.

Soon after the marriage of the young people, the worthy doctor returned to Chertsey, where, bereft of the presence of his old friends, he would have been discontented if his temperament had admitted of such a feeling, and would have turned quite peevish if he had known how. For two or three months he contented himself with hinting that he feared the air began to disagree with him; then, finding that the place really no longer was to him what it had been, he settled his business on his assistant, took a bachelor's cottage outside the village of which his young friend was pastor, and instantaneously recovered. Here he took to gardening, planting, fishing, carpentering, and various other pursuits of a similar kind, all undertaken with his characteristic impetuosity. In each and all, he has since become famous throughout the neighbourhood as a most profound authority.

Before his removal, he had managed to contract a strong friendship for Mr. Grimwig, which that eccentric gentleman cordially reciprocated. He is accordingly visited by Mr. Grimwig a great many times in the course of the year. On all such occasions Mr. Grimwig plants, fishes and carpenters with great ardour, doing everything in a very singular and unprecedented manner, but always maintaining, with his favourite asseveration, that his mode is the right one. On Sundays he never fails to criticize the sermon to the young clergyman's face, always informing Mr. Losberne, in strict confidence afterwards, that he considers it an excellent performance but deems it is as well not to say so. It is a standing and very favourite joke for Mr. Brownlow to rally him on his old prophecy concerning Oliver and to remind him of the night on which they sat with the watch between them, waiting his return; but Mr. Grimwig contends that he was right in the main, and, in proof thereof, remarks that Oliver did not come back after all—which always calls forth a laugh on his side, and increases his good humour.

ENVOI

Mr. Noah Claypole, receiving a free pardon from the Crown in consequence of being admitted approver against Fagin, and considering his profession not always as safe a one as he could wish, was for some little time at a loss for the means of a livelihood not burthened with too much work. After some consideration he went into business as an Informer, in which calling he realizes a genteel subsistence. His plan is to walk out once a week during churchtime attended by Charlotte in respectable attire. The lady faints away at the door of charitable publicans and the gentleman, being accommodated with three-pennyworth of brandy to restore her, lays an information next day and pockets half the penalty. Sometimes Mr. Claypole faints himself, but the result is the same.

Mr. and Mrs. Bumble, deprived of their situations, were gradually reduced to great indigence and misery, and finally became paupers in that very same workhouse in which they had once lorded it over others. Mr. Bumble has been heard to say that in this reverse and degradation he has not even spirit to be thankful for being separated from his wife.

As to Mr. Giles and Brittles, they still remain in their old posts, although the former is bald and the last-named boy is quite grey. They sleep at the parsonage but divide their attentions so equally among its inmates, and Oliver, and Mr. Brownlow and Mr. Losberne, that to this day the villagers have never been able to discover to which establishment they properly belong.

Master Charles Bates, appalled by Sikes's crime, fell into a train of reflection whether an honest life was not, after all, the best. Arriving at the conclusion that it certainly was, he turned his back upon the scenes of the past, resolved to amend it in some new sphere of action. He struggled hard and suffered much for some time; but having a contented disposition and a good purpose, succeeded in the end; and from being a farmer's drudge and a carrier's lad, he is now the merriest young grazier in all Northamptonshire.

And now the hand that traces these words falters as it approaches the conclusion of its task, and would weave, for a little longer space, the thread of these adventures.

I would fain linger yet with a few of these among whom I have so long moved, and share their happiness by endeavouring to depict it. I would show Rose Maylie in all the bloom and grace of early womanhood, shedding on her secluded path in life soft and gentle light, that fell on all who trod it with her, and shone into their hearts. I would paint her life and joy of the fireside circle and the lively summer group; I would follow her through the sultry fields at noon, and hear the low tones of her sweet voice in the moonlit evening walk; I would watch her in all her goodness and charity abroad, and the smiling and untiring discharge of domestic duties at home; I would paint her and her dead sister's child happy in their love of one another, and passing whole hours together in picturing the friends whom they had so sadly lost; I would summon before me, once again, those joyous little faces that clustered round her knee, and listen to their merry prattle; I would recall the tones of that clear laugh and conjure up the sympathising tear that glistened in the soft blue eye. These, and a thousand looks and smiles, and turns of thought and speech—I would fain recall them every one.

How Mr. Brownlow went on from day to day, filling the mind of his adopted child with stores of knowledge, and becoming attached to him more and more as his nature developed itself and showed the thriving seeds of all he wished him to become—how he traced in him new traits of his early friend, that awakened in his own bosom old remembrances, melancholy and yet sweet and soothing—how the two orphans, tried by adversity, remembered its lessons in mercy to others, and mutual love and fervent thanks to Him who had protected and preserved them—these are all matters that need not be told. I have said that they were truly happy; and without strong affection and humanity of heart, and gratitude to that Being whose code is mercy, and whose great attribute is benevolence to all things that breathe, happiness can never be attained.

Within the altar of the old village church there stands a white marble tablet which bears as yet but one word: 'AGNES.' There is no coffin in that tomb; and may it be many years before another name is placed above it! But if the spirits of the Dead ever come back to earth to visit spots hallowed by the love—the love beyond the grave—of those whom they knew in life, I believe that the shade of Agnes sometimes